THE WEIGHT

Joel Kauffmann

HERALD PRESS
Scottdale, Pennsylvania
Kitchener, Ontario
1980

Library of Congress Cataloging in Publication Data

Kauffmann, Joel, 1950-
   The weight.

   SUMMARY: During the turbulent summer following high
school graduation, Jon, son of a Mennonite preacher,
has to decide whether to register for the draft as a
conscientious objector or give in to peer pressure from
some of his gang and register 1-A.
   [1. Conscientious objectors — Fiction.
2. Mennonites — Fiction] I. Title.
PZ7.K164We   [Fic]   79-27262
ISBN 0-8361-1923-1

THE WEIGHT
Copyright © 1980 by Herald Press, Scottdale, Pa. 15683
   Published simultaneously in Canada by Herald Press,
   Kitchener, Ont. N2G 4M5
Library of Congress Catalog Card Number: 79-27262
International Standard Book Number: 0-8361-1923-1
Printed in the United States of America
Design by Alice B. Shetler

15 14 13 12 11 10 9 8 7 6 5 4 3 2 1

CHAPTER 1

Twe-e-e-e-t!

Coach Dudding's shrill whistle abruptly halts all activity in the gym. The coach eases himself down from his favorite resting place on the edge of the stage.

"All right," he bellows. "Everyone to the showers except . . . ." Nobody moves or breathes as the coach glares at each of us in turn. "Except Jon Springer, Steve Burky, Matt Nafzinger, Chuck Thompson, Allen Leinbach, and Denny Hill!" The rest of the gym empties immediately.

While we fidget, the coach pretends to busy himself with picking up towels and straightening papers on his clipboard. Finally he strides over to where we stand bunched together. His face starts to flush and that signals trouble.

"So, are you ready for graduation, Burky?" the coach asks in a low, even tone.

"Uh huh," Steve mumbles.

"What'd you say?"

"I said yes sir!" Steve straightens defiantly.

Bang! The sound of the coach's clipboard hitting the floor reverberates throughout the gym. "Well, I've got news for all of you. Graduation isn't until Friday night. I don't care if this is the last day of the last week of the last semester of your last year. Nobody's gonna goof off in my class!"

I can't suppress a grin. It strikes me funny to have the coach refer to gym period as a class.

"Wipe that smile off your face, Jon. Let's see how funny you think some calisthenics are. Line up!" We form a ragtag line. "Okay, push-ups from a standing position. Let's go, hands on hips. Ready . . . one, hands on floor. Two, kick back. Three, down. Four, push up. Five, kick forward. Six, stand back up . . . all the way now. Jon, take over and count." The coach's voice is crisp, like a drill sergeant, I think.

"How many, sir?" I reply in style.

"You boys think you're such good athletes, make it fifty." Coach Dudding strolls back to the stage and sits down.

"Ready, set," I call, "One, two, three, four, five—one. One, two, three, four, five—two. . . ."

"Louder, Springer, I can't *hear* you."

"ONE, TWO, THREE, FOUR, FIVE—THREE. . . ."

"C'mon Denny, you're arching your back too much," comes the voice from the stage. "Chuck, straighten all the way up on the last count. Allen, you're doing those like a girl."

". . . one, two, three, four, five—forty-nine. One, two, three, four, five—fifty." Gasps and sighs escape our sweaty, exhausted bodies. We brace hands against knees to keep from collapsing.

"Let's go. Shower up or you're gonna be late for the next class."

We drag ourselves to the stairs and stumble down the

concrete passageway to the locker room. Dudding yells after us, "Hurry it up. You guys would be in better condition if you didn't stand around so much in my class."

In the safety of the locker room, Steve whirls and gestures maliciously back in the general direction of Dudding.

We peel off our sweaty gym clothes and head for the showers. Under a warm spray of water our usual zest returns. Out of the showers, good-natured jostling quickly turns into a full-fledged towel fight. Flicks escalate to whacks and soon wet towels are raising red welts on exposed pink skin. We scamper recklessly about the locker room, overturning benches and tossing wire baskets in each other's path.

Twe-e-e-e-e-et!

The blast from Coach Dudding's whistle echoes off the concrete walls, leaving eardrums ringing. Dudding stands framed in the doorway, hands on hips, his face brilliant red.

"Clean this place up," he says. We straighten benches and replace wire baskets on shelves. "Take a seat!"

We ease gingerly onto the hard, splintery benches, defenseless against what is sure to be an onslaught. Dudding works his jaws, searching for the right words.

"Damn CO's," Dudding says almost as if he's talking to himself. "If it were up to you guys, the commies'd take over the whole world!" This opening surprises me and—I thought I was prepared for anything. I've always suspected that this issue was the source of some of Dudding's hostility toward us, but never before has it surfaced. I glance at the others. They are sitting, chins cupped in hands, staring at the bare, gray floor. Five of us are the products of Mennonite families. The sixth, Chuck,

9

comes from a family that doesn't go to Church. Chuck attends our youth group activities but has always resisted our efforts to get him to join the Mennonite Church. Dudding's condemnation of us as conscientious objectors is ironic since, for the past year, we've had an off-and-on debate among ourselves as to whether we'll ask for 1-0 status, the draft classification for conscientious objectors, or 1-A, the straight military classification—when our eighteenth birthdays arrive.

"Damn CO's," Dudding repeats more loudly, "I've had you guys three years now and I still can't understand you. You're not the first Mennonites I've taught, but you're sure as blazes the first to get uppity on me. Actin' like you're better than anybody else. Think you know more than the President himself what's right and what's wrong for this country. We're losing the Vietnam War thanks to cowards like you that can't do nothin' but criticize."

Dudding's off target here, I think. Though five of us are Mennonites, we're about as far from being peace activists as you can get without actually being in favor of war. At school, we've gone out of our way to avoid any reference to this aspect of Mennonite faith. Even when pushed we have found ways to explain our beliefs—or perhaps more accurately the beliefs of our parents—in the least offensive and controversial way. But if we could be held guilty for the fact that our parents are Mennonites, then I'm the guiltiest one of all—a preacher's kid. I've grown up with the uneasy sense that something about being Mennonite sets us apart from the rest of the world. Whatever this difference is, it now seems to be infuriating Dudding.

"What really makes me mad is that you're just a bunch of hypocrites. You talk big, you go to church on Sunday, and you skip ball practice on Wednesday night to go to some youth group, but every weekend you're out tearing around like the worst of 'em." Dudding shakes a heavy, accusing finger at us. "Oh yeah, don't think I don't know about it. Everybody knows. Your parents know but they're too protective to ever let on. Everybody knows that you go driving around picking up girls, and . . . and boozin' it up." This last remark sounds more like a question than an accusation.

The coach's words pour out rough and jumbled, but they sting. In his own way he has cut deep into my own troubled thoughts. Growing up, the label "Mennonite" always hung heavily around my neck. I've tried to ignore it, often defied it, but never have been able to shake it. Instead it has seemed to grow. Now the weight feels unbearable. My shoulders sag.

As Dudding speaks, his face grows redder and redder. He gropes for words, his thoughts choking on his own anger. "I believe in God too, y'know, and I happen to think He blessed us with a good country. A *damn* good country," he shouts stabbing the air with his forefinger. "Maybe if you was born in Russia or China . . . maybe then you'd appreciate what we got here—and not be such pansies about fightin' to keep it that way. Maybe. . . ." The words catch in his throat. "You guys make me sick, you know that? I'm glad you're graduating." Dudding practically shouts the final words, then stalks out of the locker room, slamming the door with the impact of a sonic boom.

Silence . . . and gradually nervous laughter follows his exit. Denny jumps up. "Did you see his face?" he says. "I thought he was gonna bust open—like a rotten tomato!"

"Ka-plow-ee!" Allen echoes.

While the rest get up and start to dress, I remain seated. Steve comes over and slaps me on the back. "C'mon Jon, don't let that old geezer get to you. It's no skin off your teeth."

I wince more from the sudden contact than the force of the blow. It does get to me, I think, and it is skin off my teeth—whatever that means. I'm a PK and that means getting caught between a rock and a hard place. That's the way it's always been and I'm tired of it. Tired of having to refuse to play summer baseball because the league is sponsored by the local American Legion post. Tired of feeling blamed by most of the other Mennonite kids because, then, neither could they. I'm fed up with carrying notes that excuse me from gym period while just about everyone else square danced. I am tired of being a freak, I decide. I don't want to be the angel that some would like me to be, but then again I'm not a hell-raiser either. I just want to be normal, ordinary. I want to blend in with the scenery. I'm starting to despise anything that sets me apart. Conscientious objector or soldier, what difference does it make? The war is on the other side of the world. Nothing I do . . . ."

"Get off your can, Jon!" Matt interrupts my thoughts. "We're already late for class." I dress, stuff my musty gear into my gym bag and take off after the others.

* * *

"School's out, school's out, teacher let the monkeys out." The six of us stride down the hall arm in arm, brushing aside anyone who blocks our exit. Outside we pile into the Blue Beast, an overly exotic name for Matt's worn, rusted station wagon. Being the skinniest of the

12

group, I head for my accustomed place in the center of the front seat. I slide cautiously over the threadbare seats, avoiding the springs that have begun to poke through. Denny claims the shotgun position and swings his plump form in beside me. We discard our year's accumulation of books and papers behind the rear seat onto the only luxurious feature of the car—the blue shag carpet that Matt has installed in the back.

As we roar out of the parking lot, we pass Dudding unlocking his pickup. Steve tosses a worn-out sneaker at the coach. The shoe thuds against the bumper of Dudding's truck and bounces onto the gravel. In the rearview mirror I can see Dudding shake a fist at us. Steve reaches up from the backseat and turns the mirror to comb his hair.

Matt grabs the mirror and twists it back into place. "How many times do I have to tell you guys that this mirror is for driving."

"Yeah, the way you drive," interjects Denny, "you need all the help you can get."

We crank down the windows and break into our recently adopted theme song, "Indiana Beach here we come, right back where we started from." As the mild May breeze flows through the car, we bellow this nonsense chorus at the top of our lungs. We cruise by the ancient brick buildings that line main street. Only the neon signs hanging in the store windows place the business district in the present century. We swing past the grain elevator and the old, faded houses in the center of town. Still singing, we drive leisurely past the new suburban homes on the north side of Spireville and hurry past the row of run-down shacks by the tracks west of town.

We make sure that all 1,200 residents know that three weeks after graduation we are headed for six glorious days at Indiana Beach. All we know about the place is that it is located on Lake Shafer near Monticello, Indiana. We picked it off a map of Midwestern recreational areas. The fact that we know nothing about the place makes it all the more exciting. Passing the hospital, Spireville's major attraction and my place of part-time employment in past years, our singing fades and dies. Matt turns and looks at me.

"Hey, Jon, your folks are going to let you go, aren't they?"

"Yeah," I answer. "Well, they haven't exactly said yes yet, but they'll let me." Silence. Denny reaches out and pokes Matt in the ribs.

"Don't count your chickens before they stagger from their shells. In this rattletrap of yours, none of us may make it!" We hoot and begin exchanging good-natured insults.

Allen breaks in. "Are all the plans taken care of?" A new round of hooting erupts.

"You shouldn't worry so much," Steve chides. "It makes your glasses fog up. Besides, we've got every last detail taken care of. I know how many pairs of shirts and jeans to pack. I even know how many pairs of socks I'm taking. The only thing I don't know is how many girls I'm going to make out with." The rest of us whoop in response. But, then, because it's so much fun, we go over all of our plans again, savoring every minute detail.

Finally it's time to head home. Steve, Chuck, and Allen live in town so Matt drops them off first. Next we drive Denny to his family's farm at the edge of town. Then Matt points the Blue Beast down the straight stretch of

14

blacktop toward the section of farmland where he and I are neighbors. Because of the unusually warm spring the corn in the fields on both sides of the road is already pushing to the top of the fenceposts.

Matt and I have grown up together and know each other practically inside out. I sense that the same thing that bothers me is nagging at him. I check to find out.

"How about old Dudding's speech?"

Matt gives a short laugh. "Yeah, they ought to replace his sweatshirt that says 'coach' with one that says 'God and country.' "

"But y'know," I say slowly, "in a way he's right." Matt's eyes widen. "Not about the God and country stuff—but about us. Sometimes I think we are different from everyone else—what we claim to believe about peace and all. And then at times it seems we're just the same. We do the same things, go to the same school. Nothing is different—except on Sunday we go to a different church and hear a different sermon. Do you know what I'm trying to say?"

I wish I knew what I was trying to say myself. Part of me rebels at this difference while part of me wants to cling to it. When I try to express myself about it, I feel like someone with a foot in two rowboats. My thoughts start out together, then drift further and further apart until splash—I end up in the lake.

Matt pauses while he turns onto the gravel road that leads to my house. "Yeah, sort of. There are times when I'm pretty sure about everything . . . and then times, like today, when I get mixed up." A cock pheasant flies up in front of the Blue Beast in a whoosh of wings. Matt squints, following its path as it glides down into a patch of brush. "I guess I figure I'll understand more in a couple of years. . . ."

"But we don't have a couple of years." The sudden intensity of my own voice surprises me. I continue more calmly. "I'll be 18 by the first of July and you will be in August. If we weren't going to college in the fall, they could draft us this year. Then we'd *have* to decide, wouldn't we? Even if we go to college, we'll have to figure out what we believe sometime."

"I don't know. I've heard that if the Vietnam War ends they'll be stopping the draft. That means by the time we graduate from college. . . ." Matt's voice trails off. We ride the rest of the way in silence. This has been typical of many of our discussions. Me the idealist, Matt the practical one. Maybe we won't have to face the draft, but it still seems important to know what we'd do if we had to.

Matt brings the Blue Beast to a shuddering stop in front of the simple, one-story, white-sided house where I live. I scoop up my gear and climb out.

"Hey," Matt calls after me.

"What?"

"You will get to go to Indiana Beach, won't you?"

"Yeah, sure," I reply, sounding more certain than I feel.

"Good, because my folks said that if you can't go, neither can I." Matt flashes an impish grin that betrays the fact he knows I hate being put in this position. He cranks up the window, waves, steps on the accelerator, and thunders away in a cloud of dust.

* * *

Graduation is a sentimental time when everyone conspires to drain the event of any possible emotion. Our class of 17 boys and 20 girls is outfitted in stiff robes, lined up, and marched to and fro like robots. Then we are forced to sit rigidly through the stuck-record sermon of the principal, followed by a gush of gobbledy-gook from the two members of our class who had nothing better to do than become valedictorian and salutatorian. While standing in line to receive my diploma, I look out over the audience to see if Coach Dudding is there. I can't find him.

As a final indignity, we are forced to hand over our caps to a waiting attendant immediately after receiving our diplomas. This is to prevent us from celebrating our graduation by tossing our hats into the air. "A stipulation from the cap-and-gown company," we are told.

We exit to the off-key strains of the school band struggling through "Pomp and Circumstance" without the graduating seniors. Finally we are herded off to various graduation parties and surrounded by overly admiring relatives and friends who feel compelled to ask the most personal questions they can think of. My initial resistance to probing breaks down and I confess to everything, including what year I'll get married and how many children I'll have. I even name the first born.

Afterwards, in the privacy of my room, I pull my diploma from its envelope and study it. The ornate designs of the border, the incomprehensible Latin, and the officialness of the seal all have a look of finality about them.

"A ticket to the future," the principal had said.

More like a death certificate for the first eighteen years of my life, I think to myself.

CHAPTER 2

"Ye-e-e-e-haw!"

Matt's Blue Beast roars east along Route 24. Since it's early Sunday morning, the road is clear of cars—and hopefully of police, since the speedometer quivers at eighty.

Matt, Denny, and I occupy our usual places in the front. Sitting between Chuck and Steve in the back, Allen tries to begin another round of singing. But the rest of us are sung out and refuse to join in.

The hellfire and brimstone message of a radio preacher has been fading in and out for the last several miles. Gradually it is drowned out by classical music from a nearby frequency.

According to the original plans, our week-long vacation would have begun this coming Wednesday. Normally this would have given us plenty of time before our summer job as detasseling machine drivers began. However, Denny's dad, a big wheel at the Frontier Seed Corn Company and the person responsible for getting us our jobs, had informed us that because of the early spring, detasseling would begin the last week of June. So, to get the benefit of a full week of vacation, the group had decided to start our trip three days early—on a Sunday.

My folks had been reluctant to allow me even to go on the trip—let alone to leave on a Sunday. Craftily, I had added to my other arguments the suggestion that the group would listen to an hour's worth of religious programs on the radio. My folks finally agreed, more from being worn out by my stubbornness than by the cleverness of my proposal.

Now that the classical music has completely overtaken the radio preacher, Matt reaches over to search for another station.

"Hey, watch out!" I look up just in time to see Matt flash full speed through a stop sign. The group collectively gulps.

"Hokeydina, if there'd been a car coming we'd be pancakes now!" Denny exclaims.

"Ka-plow-ee!" Allen echoes. I turn around and watch a truck fly through the intersection.

Matt locates another preacher on the radio. Soon he and I are the only ones awake to listen—Matt because he is driving and me because my conscience won't let me sleep.

"I'll be preaching today from the first book of the Bible, Genesis, the second and third chapters . . . ."

"Why do radio preachers always sound Southern and uneducated?" I muse.

"And the Lord God commanded the man, saying, 'Of every tree of the garden thou mayest freely eat: but of the tree of the knowledge of good and evil, thou shalt not eat of it: for in the day that thou eatest thereof thou shalt surely die.' "

The preacher warms up. ". . . thou shalt surely die!" he repeats. "Now the Lord didn't say, 'I will give you a headache.' He didn't say, 'I'm going to slap you on the wrist.' He didn't say, 'There'll be no TV for a week.' He said, brothers and sisters, 'Thou shalt surely die!' "

Waves of drowsiness begin to flood my mind. In this semiconscious state the reverberating voice on the radio drones on, seeming to circle about me like a vulture. "Unto the woman he said, 'I will greatly multiply thy sorrow and thy conception; in sorrow thou shalt bring forth children; and thy desire shall be to thy husband, and he shall rule over thee.' And unto Adam he said, 'Because thou hast hearkened unto the voice of thy wife, and hast eaten of the tree, of which I commanded thee, saying, Thou shalt not eat of it: cursed is the ground for thy sake; in sorrow shalt thou eat of it all the days of thy life.'

"Those of you listening out there, wherever you may be, hearken unto these words. If you have eaten from this tree of the knowledge of good and evil, I want you to fall down upon your knees, right where you are, and repent. If you have given into the temptation of the bottle, if you have been unfaithful to your partner in marriage, if you have been disobedient to your parents—whatever fruit you may have tasted—just get down on your knees and ask the Lord Jesus Christ for His forgiveness. God Almighty wants only the best for his children. He has given us a modern-day Garden of Eden in this United States of America. We call this the land of opportunity. We have good jobs, warm homes, plenty to eat, *but* the Lord God warns us that if we taste the forbidden fruits and do not repent, *We shall surely die!*"

My mind resists this emotional onslaught. Why doesn't the preacher try to help us listeners understand God instead of just scaring us? Doesn't God make sense? Or is this a test? Is God testing my faith by wanting me to accept

Him without understanding Him? But why wouldn't God want me to understand Him? If God is so great, the more we understand Him, the more we should appreciate Him. Hold on a minute! Now I'm sounding like I'm not a Christian, I think. After all, I was baptized over five years ago. Being baptized means having accepted Christ, so I must be a Christian. But then, if being a Christian means living a certain way, why am I going on this trip and planning to go along with the things the group has talked about doing?

I listen to the radio preacher again. I analyze the harshness and bitterness of the man's voice. I decide that the reason he can't help his listeners understand God is because he himself doesn't understand. If God is anything, He is love, and there is not a shred of love or compassion in this guy's voice. God couldn't be as cruel or as vengeful as the radio voice would like his listeners to believe.

The preacher comes to the end of his message. "I have written a pamphlet entitled *The Forbidden Fruits* that I would like for all of you listeners to have. This book is absolutely free. There is no cost to you, and in a minute I'll give you the address to write to. But first I want to remind you that this broadcast is made possible only through the faithful support I have received from you listeners who have heard the Word and hearkened unto it. So those of you that have been touched by. . . ." Sleep comes mercifully.

* * *

"Twenty miles to Indiana Beach!" The occupants of the Blue Beast stir, stretch, and come to life.

"Hey, Matt, run any more stop signs?"

"None that I know of. Course I slept awhile myself."

"I'm starved. What time is it?" Denny asks.

"Hold on till we get there. We can ask some girls where the best restaurants are."

"Yeah, then we can look for the cheapest."

"Cheap, schmeep! Everything's first class this week."

"Right now I've got first-class hunger pains."

"Here, my Mom gave me some cookies to eat on the way." Six hands reach for the bag and the cookies quickly vanish.

"Hey!" Steve shouts, leaning forward, "I have an idea."

"Finish your cookie first. You're spitting crumbs all over me."

"Yeah, all your ideas are half-baked anyhow." This is true. Steve is always coming up with cornball suggestions that end up getting somebody in trouble—usually somebody other than himself. Like the time he suggested building a clubhouse. He claimed he knew where we could get free wood. We had the clubhouse half built before we found out that the wood belonged to a farmer who lived next to Matt and myself. The farmer had torn down an old barn and was storing the wood to build an implement shed. Because Matt and I lived the closest, we took most of the heat. Then there was the time that Steve had convinced us all to wear shabby clothes to school in violation of the dress code. He argued that we would be protesting an oppressive and meaningless regulation. Unfortunately, the day of the protest, Steve came down with a cold and wasn't in school.

But now, Steve won't be surpressed. "The way I figure it," he lowers his voice dramatically, "we'll be doing all kinds of things this week."

"What kind of things?"

"Oh, all kinds. Most of the stuff we do might be okay, but . . ." Steve pauses. By now we are hooked. "Well the way I figure it, if we were to do something really far-out, and it got back to our parents, we could get burnt pretty bad. So I say, let's each come up with a code name instead of our real ones. Then nobody can trace a thing back to us." Steve has the knack of making something completely crazy sound not only exciting but downright logical.

"Great!" Denny jumps in. "If we use code names, we can pull off all kinds of junk and nobody will be the wiser." No one bothers with the fact that we'd still be carrying our driver's licenses on us. Steve sits back triumphantly while the rest of our minds take off.

We spend the last few miles of the trip choosing and memorizing the code names we'll use at Indiana Beach. Chuck picks Clark Kender, a take-off of Superman's alias. Matt, the best athlete of the group, chooses Lefty Grove. Steve, the dark-complexioned lady killer, insists on Juan Caldron. Denny, the comedian picks the initials W. C. And Allen, the bright one, selects the most sophisticated handle he can muster—Bennett Lawson. When my turn comes, I say the first name that pops into my mind—Bob Dudding, the name of our ex-coach. I immediately regret the choice. The others go into convulsions imagining me in various situations.

"Hey," Steve chortles, "I got one. Imagine walking up to this girl and having to say, 'Hello there, beautiful, my name in DUD-ding.' " Laughter.

"Or," Denny adds, "getting stopped by a cop and being asked what your name is. 'Du-Du-Du-Du-Du-Dudding, sir.' " More hilarity.

We crest a hill and Lake Shafer stretches before us in a

thin, silver band. Matt lays on the horn. We roll down the windows and break into our final and most vigorous rendition of "Indiana Beach, here we come."

"Restaurant on the right!" Matt jams on the brakes. The Blue Beast fishtails, slows, and swings into a parking lot under a sign that reads, "Woody's Cafe." We pile out of the car and stampede inside to a table. When the clattering of our chairs dies down, a waitress brings us menus.

Steve scans his menu. "Well, well, a fine selection. What'll you have, Clark?" Chuck doesn't respond. Steve nudges him in the ribs.

"Uh, oh yeah," Chuck stutters, "a real fine selection. I think I'll have a hamburger . . . . No, make it a . . . a . . . Somebody else order first."

Denny rummages in his wallet. "I don't want to break a ten," he says. "Do you have anything that costs exactly a dollar and seventeen cents?" Laughter. The waitress begins to shift from foot to foot.

"What about you, Dudding?" Steve asks. "I see they have some chocolate *pudding*."

"Pudding for Dudding. Dudding pudding," the others chime in.

"I'll come back when you've made up your minds." The waitress withdraws into the kitchen. A few minutes later the manager appears.

"I'm glad you fellows are enjoying yourselves, but please keep it down for the sake of the other customers."

Denny pipes up, "If they can keep their food down, we can keep ours down." We crack up. The manager glares at us.

"Another remark like that and I'll have to ask you to leave."

24

Steve bristles, "You'd better start talking nicer to your customers or I'll tell Woody on you."

"I am Woody."

Denny cannot resist his Woody Woodpecker impression.

"That does it. Out!"

"In that case, do you have carry-outs?" Steve asks.

Woody points to a sign above the cash register. "You see that sign? It says I can refuse service to anyone at any time. That's so hot-shots like you can't ruin things for everyone else. Now are you leaving or do I call the cops?" The rest of the dining room has grown deathly quiet.

"We'll leave, we'll leave," Steve speaks loudly starting to get up. "We'd probably get food poisoning if we ate in this flea trap anyhow." As Steve reaches for his sunglasses, he knocks over a glass of water. I stand up feeling the blood run hot in my cheeks. Steve stomps out and the rest of us follow.

Back in the car Steve's in an ugly mood. "Who does that old fogy think he is?" When Steve gets like this, only Chuck can stand up to him.

"C'mon Steve, cool off. We'll starve to death if we keep getting kicked out of restaurants."

"Yeah," Matt adds, "If I was him, I'd have done the same thing."

"He'll get his, if I have anything to say about it," Steve vows. "He'll get his."

By now Denny is desperate with hunger. "Look, up on the left, a McDonalds." We pull into fast-food land and gorge ourselves on bland hamburgers, shakes, and fries. But it means a full stomach—and soon the carload's in good spirits again.

"What do we do now?"

"First, let's find a place to stay. We need to dump some of this luggage to make room for picking up girls." We cheer the idea and Matt heads the Blue Beast along the row of boarding houses and cottages that line the shorefront.

"Pull over. That looks good." The Blue Beast grinds to a halt in front of a green-shingled, three-story apartment complex. We pour out of the car and encircle the building.

"This place doesn't even have an office," Matt yells. We knock on doors until a middle-aged woman answers.

"Pardon us," Steve begins eloquently, "but my friends and I are looking for a place in which to reside while on vacation at this pleasant resort."

The woman smiles. "I'm sorry, but I'm just a renter."

"Then could you please tell us how we might find the manager?"

"I'm afraid the manager doesn't live around here."

"Then how might we get in touch with him?"

"It's a lady, actually. All my contact with her is by mail. I reserve the apartment that way and send her the rent money. I don't think it would do you any good, though, even if you could get hold of her. These apartments are usually booked well in advance."

"I see . . . . Well, uh, thank you for your time then."

"That's perfectly all right." The woman smiles and closes the door.

"Old bag," Steve mutters as we head back to the car.

We spend the rest of the afternoon combing the beach front without success. Most rooms are already rented out. At the few that are available, we are told that we are too young. One owner curtly informs us that he doesn't rent to males.

"Pardon our hormones," Denny grumbles.

At a scruffy cafe where we eat supper, the proprietor mentions some cottages a mile-and-a-half off the beach that he thinks will be available. We wolf down our hot dogs, pile into the car, and chase down the lead. We find the cottages and immediately understand why they're available. The paint has long worn off the sides. The roof is missing shingles. Windows are cracked or covered with cardboard.

"Can I help you?" We turn to face a spooky-eyed old man in tattered coveralls.

"Yeah," Chuck volunteers. "We're looking for a place to stay. You got any places left?"

The old man makes a panoramic sweep with his hand.

"Could we see one?"

"Your best one," Steve adds.

"Sure thing," he says. "Barney's the name." Barney shakes hands with each of us in turn. He digs deep into the side pocket of his coveralls and pulls out a heavy key chain. He motions to us and we follow him to a nearby cabin. At the door he sorts through the numerous keys, cursing under his breath.

"There." The door gives way and swings open with an ominous creak. Barney reaches in and turns on the single bare light bulb that hangs from a cord in the center of the room. As light floods the room I can see tiny creatures scurry for the cracks in the floorboards. My stomach turns as I survey the garbage-strewn room. I glance at the faces of the others and see uniformly ill expressions.

"Well, whaddya say? It's not much but it'll keep the rain off your nose an' the frost off your toes."

We all turn to Steve. "I tell you what," he says, "we'll talk it over, but first we have some errands to run." Steve motions to the rest of us and we rush for the car.

"I'll be waitin' right here," Barney calls after us.

"Don't hold your breath," Chuck mutters. Matt spins gravel as he takes off.

"What do we do now?"

"I don't know," Steve replies, "but it's a sure bet we won't pay good money for a dump like that."

"What do we need a place for anyhow? We have sleeping bags. Let's just sack out on the beach."

"Where'll we take the girls?"

"We'll go to their place." So it's decided to call off our search for living quarters. We drive back to the resort. The "resort" consists mostly of a dilapidated, half-mile boardwalk lined with eating places, carnival rides, and shops full of foreign-made trinkets. Being Sunday night, the walk is deserted except for a few strays like ourselves and the gray-suited security men. The guards seem to eye us with suspicion as we walk along.

"Man, it's like we're breaking some kind of law or something," Denny complains. We find a cluster of pinball machines and pass the remainder of the evening shooting balls and flipping levers. We happen upon one machine that gives free replays everytime if the reset button is pushed just before the last ball drops.

"Beach curfew in five minutes." The stern voice comes from behind us.

"We're planning to sleep on the beach," I inform the guard.

"Not on your life," the guard retorts.

"Why not?"

"It's illegal."

"Who says it's illegal?" Chuck asks.

"The sign says it's illegal."

"We see that, but who made the stupid rule in the first place?"

"Look kid, the sign says it's against the law, so it's against the law. You've now got three minutes to get off the premises." Chuck shrugs and we casually stroll back to the car. We get in and head off to find a place to spend the night. Unfortunately nearly every square foot of land in Indiana Beach seems to be in use for cottages, taverns, gas stations, or grocery marts.

We turn a corner and the headlights illuminate some trees.

"Over there. A grassy area!"

"I don't believe it." Cheering, we park the car, pile out, unroll our sleeping bags, and crawl in.

Bzzzzz. Slap! Bzzzzz. Slap! Slap!

"Hey!" Allen cries, "I'm being eaten alive!"

"So am I. Me too," we all echo. For another five minutes we fight off the invisible creatures. But the more we flail and swat, the more mosquitoes we attract.

"Forget this bull," I yell. "I'm sleeping in the car." Another chorus of "me too's."

We shift and squirm in the car trying to find a comfortable spot. One by one the others drop off to sleep. Soon Allen and I are the only ones still awake.

Plink, plunk.

"Oh, no—rain." Allen and I break out in restrained laughter.

"Well," I observe, "at least it'll drown the mosquitoes."

"Imagine a nice warm bed with clean sheets," Allen fantasizes.

"And room to stretch out," I add. I squirm one final time, then drift off to the relentless rhythm of the falling rain.

CHAPTER 3

"What time is it?"

"Six-thirty."

"Morning or evening?"

"Morning. Go back to sleep." I twist my cramped body trying to find a position that will allow me another hour of rest.

"What time is it?"

"Seven-thirty."

"Morning or evening?" It could be either one. The sky is overcast with a solid gray blanket. The rain has subsided to a light drizzle. The cramped quarters of the Blue Beast are damp from the humidity in the air and sweat from sleeping so close together. One by one we awaken, crawl out, and look around.

"No wonder there were so many mosquitoes last night," Allen calls. "We were sleeping by a creek."

"Creek, my foot," Steve hollers from further away. "This is a stinkin' sewer!" He pulls a wooden sign out of the ground and holds it up for us to see. It reads, "Danger: Open Drainage Ditch." Steve tosses the sign into the sludge and races back to the car. We pile in and take off as fast as we can.

We stop at a small, dingy cafe for breakfast. Between bites of food we discuss what to do next. Steve finishes off a piece of toast. "I say we go back and take a cabin at Barney's."

"What?"

"I thought you didn't like that dump."

"Like has nothing to do with it. It's a cinch we can't sleep out in the rain or along a sewer."

"Yeah, at least we'd have a place to dump our gear," Chuck chips in.

"Anyhow," I add, "we'll just be spending the nights there."

"We could clean the place up," Allen suggests.

"You can if you want," Chuck retorts, "I'm not spending my vacation cleaning up anything."

"Unless it's cleaning up on all the girls at the beach," Steve leers. We finish breakfast and drive back to Barney's.

As we pull in, Barney appears in the doorway of the cottage he had shown us yesterday. Wearing a faded apron over his coveralls, he holds a frayed broom in one hand and a dustpan in the other.

"Good mornin' boys," he calls out. "Your cabin is waitin' for you." We file in and look around. The garbage has been picked up and taken out. The floor still isn't clean, but at least the dirt looks rearranged. The old cots and chairs have been pushed against the cabin's walls.

"How much?" Steve asks.

"Twelve bucks a day, cash. That includes the bathroom out back." We follow his gaze to a crooked shanty, half-hidden in the weeds.

"We'll try it for one day." Steve collects two dollars from each of us and hands the loot to Barney who crumples and shoves it into his shirt.

"Don't believe I caught your names," Barney queries.

"St—uh, Juan Caldron," Steve begins. Barney raises an eyebrow.

"Clark Kender."

"Bennett Lawson."

"Lefty Grove."

"W.C."

"W.C. what?"

"Just W.C."

"Oh." Barney looks at me.

"Bob Dudding."

"That's not a very exciting name."

"I'm sorry."

"Nothing to be sorry about. If that's what your folks named you, it's not your fault. At least they gave you a complete name." Barney begins to amble away. "Well, if there's anything you boys need, I'll be within hollerin' distance," he calls over his shoulder.

We unload our gear from the car and haul it into the cabin. We decide on a sleeping arrangement and begin to unpack.

"There goes a cockroach."

"I thought he cleaned this dump out."

"Here . . . ." Chuck grabs an old magazine. "I'll take care of it."

"No." Steve grabs his arm. "There's a jar on the shelf. Let's catch it. We can keep it as a pet."

"You're crazy. A cockroach? I say let's kill it."

"It's not the bug's fault this place is a dump." Steve grabs the heavy glass jar and takes off after the roach. After a short but furious chase, he traps the insect. Denny finds a piece of tin foil to cover the jar.

Allen shakes his head. "I've heard of crazy pets—but a filthy cockroach?"

Steve sets the jar carefully on the shelf. "I think it gives the place atmosphere," he chuckles. "And besides, it might even turn out to be useful."

* * *

Monday remains cold and misty. We cruise the resort, but if there are people around they are sane enough to stay inside their cabins.

Tuesday is rainy and even colder. Even we stay inside. We spend the morning napping on our cots which are now arranged to avoid the numerous drips from the roof.

"We're getting a head start on all the sleep we'll be missing the rest of the week," Denny ventures optimistically.

Only Steve keeps himself occupied. He darts back and forth across the cabin floor capturing roaches that have infiltrated the cabin to escape the rain. The jar on the shelf now swarms with the black creatures. Steve responds to all questions about his activity with the same vague reply: "Oh, you just never know when you're going to need a jar full of cockroaches."

Cards and conversation help pass the afternoon. We brave the drips and arrange our cots in a circle. We lie on our stomachs facing the center.

"C'mon Allen, deal," Denny snaps. "If you shuffle any longer, you're gonna wear the ink off those cards."

"At least I get them mixed up."

"You saying I don't shuffle right?"

"Only if you don't mind playing the same hand twice."

"Hurry up, will you?"

"What's the rush, we got all day."

"Hey, Dudding." I ignore the salutation. "Hey, Dudding," Steve repeats.

"You talking to me?" I ask, looking up. The Dudding stuff is starting to irritate me.

"Yeah, your birthday's coming up in July, isn't it?"

I yawn. "Early July. What about it?"

"What are you going to do about the draft?"

"Close the window," says Denny to a chorus of hisses at this old joke.

"No, really."

I look at Steve to make sure he's serious. Steve often starts arguments just for the fun of arguing.

"I don't know." I reply casually. "I haven't given it much thought." A lie. Lately I've worried about it a lot—poring over manuals and pamphlets, comparing my fledgling convictions with those of others.

"What's to think about? You're either going to go 1-A or 1-0."

Steve is trying to bait me. It's nothing personal. Mainly a way to beat the boredom. "What're *you* going to do?" I turn the question.

"That's why I'm asking you. I figure you being a PK and all . . . maybe the rest of us can get some pointers."

I don't want to respond but Steve has pushed me to the place where I have to say something. Knowing that he and Chuck have always been the most militaristic of our group, I choose the other side for argument's sake. Mustering more conviction than I feel, I say: "Unless something changes my mind before I sign up, I'm going to ask for a 1-0 classification." The card playing stops.

"What made you decide?" asks Matt.

"Nothing special." I try to sound nonchalant. "It just

34

seems strange to me that people expect you to go and kill people unless you have a good reason *not* to. The way I look at it, unless I have a good reason *to* go into the army and kill, I'd just as soon stay out and do something else. I just haven't thought of a good reason to kill anyone yet."

"What if someone attacked your mother?" Steve asks.

"I don't have to join the army to defend my mother."

Steve presses. "Okay, what about if some nation attacks this country? You'd just let them take it over?"

"Who's going to attack this country? We haven't been attacked for over 150 years."

"Yeah, and that's because we've built the biggest military force in the world. If everyone thought like you, any dinky country in the world could come over and whip us in a day's time."

"If everyone thought like me, no country would want to come over and whip us. Besides, not everyone thinks like me. If people want to go into the army, they have a right to." We've been through variations of this argument countless times. The next question will be, "Then why should those who go into the army defend people like you who refuse to fight?" After that, the logic will become snarled and shatter into a thousand pieces.

Matt breaks in. "Better not let Dudding hear you talk like that." I glance at him and see, to my relief, that he's kidding.

"Yeah," Denny cracks, "he'll make you give his name back." Everyone joins in a round of tension-relieving laughter.

"Hey, there goes another one!" Steve spots a scurrying roach and gives chase. Everyone seems to forget the discussion except me. In a way I feel like I've blown another chance to help the gang come to some kind of decision. If I could just once put the right words together. Why aren't the answers simpler? Who knows, maybe the answers are simple and I'm too dense to understand. My mood turns glum.

All of a sudden Denny goes bananas. "Girls!" he roars. "I haven't even seen a girl for twenty-four hours." The gang rallies to the battle cry and we head for the Blue Beast. We cruise the misty streets around the resort but they remain virtually desolate. Even our pinball machine has been carted away for repairs. No more free games.

* * *

"The sun's coming up! The sun's coming up!" Allen's maniacal screams rouse the rest of us.

"Tell it to go back down," Chuck mumbles groggily. Soon, however, the realization of a sunny day hits us, and we scramble from our rumpled bags.

"Ye-e-e-haw!" Steve grabs his jar of roaches and holds them out in the sunlight. "What do you think of that, my little friends?" They obviously don't think much of it and he returns them to their dark shelf.

"What are we going to do about breakfast?" Denny asks.

"Forget food. All we've done for three days is sleep and eat. Let's hit the beach." We grab our swimming gear, pack a few essentials, and make a beeline for the resort.

We arrive early but already we see more people than we've encountered for the last three days combined. They stream forth from everywhere. Cabin doors open and middle-aged couples with frenzied kids come pouring out. Vans deliver scores of teen and college-age youth. Older couples amble from cottages and carefully set their beach chairs under umbrellas.

"Never could figure out why anyone would come to the beach for sun and then sit in the shade," Steve says.

"Look at all the people!" Chuck exclaims. "I mean, would you just *look* at all those beautiful people!" He throws his hands in the air and starts dancing circles in the sand.

"Last one in the water buys dinner." Towels fly and the sand churns beneath our feet. We all hit the lake at once. The water is cold but no one admits it. We swim, dive, play tag, and start water fights. The morning passes quickly.

"I'm famished," Denny says. The rest of us realize that we are, too. We head for shore and towel off. I hunt for my billfold and remember I left it at the cabin. Allen offers to lend me some money but I don't want my billfold left unattended in an unlocked cabin. Matt gives me the keys to the Blue Beast. The others remember various odds and ends that they want from their belongings. I make a list.

"Don't take all the girls while I'm gone," I call as I head for the car.

"First come, first served," Steve hollers back. Everything and everyone is rosy today. Life is as it should be. I feel light-hearted and free—just the way grown-ups and television commercials tell us teenage kids should. Yesterday's anxieties have dissolved in the warm, soothing rays of the sun. I decide the weather must have been my problem yesterday. Everything seems worse when it's cold and rainy.

I make the mile-and-a-half trip quickly, rush into the cabin, and begin scooping up the requested items. I dig through Allen's neatly packed suitcase for his suntan lotion.

"How's it going?" a voice behind me booms. Startled, I nearly hit the rafters.

"Sorry, didn't mean to scare you," Barney laughs. He comes in and sits on the edge of a cot.

Oh, no, I think to myself. I don't have time to talk now. I have to get back.

"You boys havin' a good time?"

"Yeah, it's a great day out there."

"Be-e-e-eautiful day," Barney exclaims. He settles back. "I tell you, this Hoosier weather's the strangest thing. One day it's rainin' and the next it'll shine like you're in the desert itself. Never met a man that could predict it."

Great, a conversation about the weather, I think to myself. If I don't get back soon, it may well start to rain again. I find Allen's lotion and edge toward the door.

"You boys are stayin' out of trouble, aren't you?" I look at Barney to see if he's kidding. The expression on his face and the sudden change of tone in his voice convince me that he's not.

"We haven't had a chance to get into any yet," I grin. The somber expression on Barney's face remains.

"In my business, I've learned how to judge character—and I'd say that you fellows is good boys. One of you may even have a preacher for a pappy." A slight chill runs through me. Barney continues, " I wouldn't want to see any good youngsters like yourselves get in any kind of trouble. And believe me, a feller can find trouble in these here parts."

I break in, trying to stop Barney before his sermon gets up to full steam. "Well," I blurt, "we don't plan on getting into trouble." I step closer to the door—and freedom.

Barney keeps going. "You may not believe it, but once

I was a good boy. Never missed a day of school or church till I was fourteen. My pappy was a preacher in a little mission church over across town." Barney pauses to choke back a sob.

I'm trapped. I have to ask, "What happened?"

Barney's story gushes forth. "My pappy ran off with a widow lady from church. My ma just stayed home nights acryin' and aweepin'. Nothin' seemed to do much good. One day I just couldn't take it no more, so I took off and began arunnin' around with all sorts of riffraff. Never went back to church or school ever again. Took to drinkin' and asmokin' and agamblin' and carousin' like you never did see. Thought I was the biggest thing this side of the Mississippi. . . ." Barney sighs and stands up. "Well, I reckon I'm keepin' you from your friends."

I nod mutely and hurry out the door.

"Stay out of trouble now," Barney calls after me.

Driving back to the beach I try to shake off the incident. I am irritated at Barney for spoiling my day with his troubles, and angry at myself for not wanting to take the time to listen. Why *should* I feel guilty? I think. I don't owe him anything. We're just renting his cabin.

I find the gang stretched out on blankets soaking up sun. "What took you so long?" Allen asks as I walk up.

"If you guys wouldn't have given me a shopping list a mile long, I'd have been back in no time flat." I decide to let it go at that.

We dine on soggy hamburgers from a beach-side stand. We walk off the indigestion by touring the trinket stands. My usual thriftiness breaks down and I blow five bucks on a ridiculous red hat with "Indiana Beach" printed on in huge white letters.

Full stomachs and a hot afternoon sun make us drowsy.

We head back to the beach for a snooze. I fall asleep counting bikini-clad girls jumping over sand castles to block the image of Barney from my mind.

"Somebody turn Jon over so he get's done on both sides." I hear my name and wake up. The rest are up and putting on T-shirts.

"Let's rustle up some eager chicks," Steve suggests. "We've got enough sun for one day."

We start our search by splitting up into twos. Steve pairs off with Chuck. Allen goes with Denny. Matt and I head down the beach together.

We keep our eyes open and plan strategy. I spot two girls sunning themselves in a rental rowboat, hit upon an idea, and inform Matt.

We dive into the water and swim out as close to the boat as we dare without being heard or spotted. We dive under and swim past the rowboat as far as we can. When our lungs are bursting, we surface. Swimming back toward the girls, I wave my hand and yell.

"Help! My buddy has a cramp." The girls sit up, then quickly row over to meet us. With their assistance I "help" Matt aboard. While he clutches his right leg, I explain to the fair maidens that we began swimming from the other shore in an effort to cross the lake. The girls are impressed. We explain how, in the last fifty feet, the cold water caused the muscles in Matt's leg to tighten up. For effect Matt begins rubbing his left calf.

"Oh, that's too bad," the girls sympathize. They whisper something to each other that I can't make out.

"Y'know," one of them says, "the best way to relax your muscles is to put your legs back in the water and let someone massage them. Here, you sit on the edge, let your legs dangle in the water, and I'll give you a good rubdown," she instructs Matt.

The other one turns to me. "What about you?" she asks. I'll bet your muscles were getting stiff too."

"Well now that you mention it. . . ." I grimace. She helps me into position.

"Now!" On a signal the girls dump us foward into the water. By the time we surface and shake the water from our eyes, they are rowing away.

"Next time either of you guys gets a cramp," one of them calls, "try to remember which leg it's in."

Matt and I swim slowly back to shore, planning the story we'll tell the other guys.

CHAPTER 4

"Steve, either take care of these bugs or get rid of them." Allen holds up the jar of cockroaches. I walk over and take a look. The roaches are in atrocious condition. Severed legs and feelers cling to the inside of the dank jar. Dead roaches lie belly up on the bottom while comrades greedily devour them. A fetid odor escapes the punched holes in the tin foil.

I join the complaint. "The least you could do is give them something to eat—besides each other."

Steve continues to squint into the cracked, smokey mirror on the wall. He brushes his slick, jet-black hair and adjusts his lapels for the hundredth time. "Don't get all bent out of shape," he replies. "They'll be gone by tomorrow morning."

"So will we!" Allen disgustedly replaces the jar on the shelf and scrubs his hands at the sink.

Tonight is the big night. Friday night, we've been told by many reputable sources, is the night Indiana Beach comes alive. Guys and gals from miles around congregate at the night spots. "A gorilla with acne and a lisp could score at Indiana Beach on a Friday night," one person had told us.

42

This is our last night at the resort and we plan to make the most of it. We are all showered, shaved, and shined. Unfortunately, only Allen thought to bring along cologne, so we all smell of his English Leather. Each of us is dressed in the only good set of clothes he brought—neatly pressed, packed, and preserved for this climactic moment.

Chuck and Steve good-naturedly argue strategy. "I say find one decent girl and stick with her no matter what," Chuck exclaims.

"No way," Steve retorts in his man-of-the-world manner. "If the first one is a lemon, then you've blown the whole night. You got to use the buckshot approach. Keep picking them up and dropping them until you hit the jackpot."

Denny jumps into the ruckus. "My theory is, go for the homely ones," he proclaims.

"You would say that," Allen guffaws. The rest of us jeer loudly.

"Now wait a minute," Denny continues. "The way I figure it, you're not going to marry her, right? I mean you're just after a little lovin'. Well, you get some good-looking, stuck-up chick and you'll end up nowhere. But, get some desperate broad . . ."

"Maybe we'll get hold of some hooch," Steve says. "Then it won't make any difference."

We pile out of the cabin and into the Blue Beast.

Barney sits whittling on a bench in front of his clapboard house. He glances up for a second, then his gaze returns to the stick he is working on. I give a feeble wave that he doesn't acknowledge. I breathe easier when we are out of sight of the cabins.

Two girls walk along the road. We roll down the

windows, hang out our heads, and pass them with whistles which they ignore.

A hitchhiker thumbs in our direction. Matt slows down. "Wanna lift?" Denny calls out. The hitchhiker starts for our car. "Lift that billboard," Denny hollers, pointing at a sign. Matt peels away as we break into gales of laughter.

The boardwalk is crammed and overflowing with people. The night spots won't open for another two hours. We stroll up and down the walk eating popcorn, trying our luck at games of chance, and advertising our availability.

We spot an open manhole and decide to pull a version of our favorite prank. We gather around the hole and stare intently into the depths. Soon a small crowd collects around us, attracted by curiosity. On cue we point down into the hole and yell in mock terror, "Look out, it's coming up!" Children shriek and the crowd scatters in momentary panic.

"You, sonny. Yes, you. You look like a football player. What position do you play, halfback?" The barker's flattery works and I'm a dollar poorer. While I try my luck at ringing the bell with a big wooden mallet, Steve drifts away from the group. When I finish my last try, unsuccessfully, he is back and huddled with the rest of the gang. Eagerly Steve beckons for me to join them.

"Hey," he repeats for me. "That guy over there says he'll sell us half a case of beer." I follow Steve's finger to a shirtless man with greasy hair and a tattooed chest.

"Well, what do you say?"

I don't respond.

"The rest of us will go along if you do. We all have to be in on it, though."

I look over at Matt. He shrugs and looks away.

"C'mon, Jon," Chuck prods. "That's only two cans apiece. A couple of beers won't kill you. In fact, they say a little beer is good for you."

Here I am on the spot again, I think to myself. Why should I be the one to say no if everyone else wants to? I nod slightly. That's all Steve needs.

"All right!" Steve slaps me on the back and rushes over to confer with the greasy stranger. Soon he returns.

"He says we're to get in our car and follow him out of town. He knows a spot where we can pay him and exchange the stuff."

We follow the stranger's heavy black Pontiac past rows of cottages and grocery marts until we come to a small wooded section.

The stranger pulls onto a dirt lane and comes to a stop in a small clearing. The transaction is quickly made. When Steve comes back, he is carrying a full case. He reports that the stranger agreed to sell us the whole case in a sudden burst of good will. I suspect that the full case was in the deal all along. The stranger toots and roars out of the clearing, leaving us by ourselves.

Steve tears the cardboard off the case and pulls out a can. It's malt liquor, twice as potent as regular beer. Steve whoops and pops the tab. He throws his head back and chugs. He stops red-eyed and sputtering. Booze runs down his chin, soaking his shirt. He wrings his shirt out over the can in a comical effort to save every drop of the precious liquid.

Suddenly I remember Dudding's accusation the last day of school in the locker room. "Everybody knows that you go driving around picking up girls, and boozin' it up."

Dudding would have made a good prophet, I think.

I open the can Chuck hands me and take a sip.

Involuntarily, my throat contracts and I spit the fiery liquid onto the ground. No wonder the guy wanted to get rid of the stuff. It tastes like it's gone bad—unless that's the way malt liquor actually tastes.

"What's the matter?" Steve goads. "Can't you handle it?"

I take another swallow, forcing the burning brew down my throat. I barely avoid regurgitating it. My progress is slow. Each swallow must combat the better instincts of my mind and body. Steve finishes his second can and Chuck opens a third. This is ridiculous, I tell myself. A little of this isn't going to hurt me. Besides, how will I ever know drinking is wrong unless I try it? This could actually be an educational experience, I convince myself.

I take a larger gulp. I shake the can. Still over half full. At this rate, I think, I'll be here all night with one can. I brace my body. Ready? Here goes. I tilt my head back and suck the can dry.

Fireworks explode inside of me. A forest fire engulfs my stomach, sending flames to every part of my body. My brain fights to stay coherent but quickly succumbs to the incinerating heat. Then the fire subsides, leaving only a warm, mellow glow.

The second can is tolerable. I drink it slowly, chugging only the bottom quarter of its contents. The third actually tastes good. The last can goes too quickly. I search the debris for more but all the cans have long been drained.

With the liquor gone, we link arms and begin singing our school's fight song:

> On Spireville, on Spireville,
> We are proud of thee-e-e-e.
> Send that ball right through the basket.

Fight for victory, rah, rah, rah!
On Spireville, on Spireville,
Spiral to the stars.
If we fight for truth and ri-i-ight,
Victory will be ours.

Chorus after chorus we sing. Arms intertwined we stumble unsteadily among the clearing, entertaining our audience of trees, brush and discarded litter. We end the last chorus standing on the roof of the Blue Beast kicking our legs out in time to the music.

Crunch! The roof buckles and we tumble to the ground. Struggling to our feet, we laugh and brush ourselves off. Chuck finds a large, smooth rock, crawls inside the car, and bangs the roof back approximately into its original shape.

Allen leans against the car and squints at his watch. "Hey," he slurs, "the dance starts in half an hour." We stumble and fall into the car. Denny rips his pants on a spring.

Matt spins around the clearing cutting kitties. I hold an arm out the window and pretend I'm flying. I draw it back after I nearly lose it to a sapling. The bark of another tree succeeds in taking blue paint and rust from the front fender.

Matt heads out the dirt lane and back down the highway to the resort. The road has become as wide open as a parking lot. Matt careens all over it. Other drivers too selfish to share the space honk and blink their lights at us as they pass.

"Sunday drivers," growls Matt.

The drab boardwalk has been transformed into a fairyland during our absence. The chipped paint and scruffy people have disappeared. They have been

47

replaced by magnificent, multicolored lights, bright cheerful music, delicious odors, and fairy princesses. Only the occasional black knights are to be feared. Steve warns us about the dark-suited security men who will take us to their dungeons if they spot and catch us. When one appears, we straighten up and march along like pious choirboys, doing our best to stay in a straight line along the boardwalk that keeps swaying from side to side.

Off in the distance, we hear the rumble and twang of electronic instruments being tuned. "Hey, the dance is starting!" Allen exclaims. We stagger off in the direction of the sounds.

"Excuse us, excuse us," we say as we break through clusters of people that seem to be moving in slow motion. The people turn and frown at us. Their faces seem distorted, their noses incredibly long.

"Hey, what's happening baby?" Steve throws his arm around a girl who was separated from her companions by our group. She fights off his embrace and hurries to her friends. A guard notices the incident and steps in front of us, cutting off our path.

"You boys okay?" he asks sternly.

Act normal, act normal, my mind screams. I have sudden visions of my parents being called up long-distance and told that their son is in jail.

But we're fortunate. "You boys have your fun," the guard says. "But," his voice hardens, "don't go bothering anyone else. Y'hear?"

"Yesshir," we mumble and hurry away. I feel humiliated. Like the time I was talking in church and Dad stopped his sermon to tell me to straighten up.

At the dance, we pay the door charge and have our left hands stamped with fluorescent ink. We enter the black womb of the dance hall. Strangely colored lights blink to the pulsating rhythm of the band that has begun to play. The floor is jammed with silhouetted figures. A few are dancing; most stand motionless. We stumble through the dark statues until we come to a clear space along a wall. A shadowy figure nearby silently offers Steve a red-glowing cigarette. Steve takes a puff and passes it to Chuck. Chuck inhales and gives it to me. The brownish cylinder emits a strange, sweet odor.

"What's this?" I wonder aloud. The figure grabs it from me and disappears.

Steve gives me a disgusted look. "C'mon," he suggests, "let's split up. We'll never get any girls standing around like this." Steve and Chuck head off one way and Allen and Denny go the other.

Standing with Matt, everything seems unreal and comical. "Who would've guessed a year ago," I slur, "that we'd be standing at this very spot, stoned out of our minds?" We break into uncontrollable giggles.

Two girls approach us. "What're you guys doing?" one of them asks.

"Just waiting for you," I reply as suavely as I can. We pair off and head for the dance floor. I've only danced twice in my life and felt foolish both times. But now I'm loose and I dance ecstatically. A natural born dancer, I tell myself, ignoring the bemused look on my partner's face.

"Thanks for the dance. See you around," I say when the dance is over. I steer Matt away from the girls.

"What's wrong with you?" he asks. "We should've stuck with them awhile. They seemed okay."

"The wrong type. Too forward."

"What's the right type," he mutters. "The kind you have to peel off a wall?"

"I'll let you know when we find some," I reply. The effects of the booze make me feel in charge and, for now, I am enjoying it. I walk up to a pair of girls relaxing on a bench.

"Care to dance?" I inquire.

"We'll have to ask our boyfriends first," one replies. I move on to a cluster of girls standing off to one corner. I decide to try a more forceful approach.

"I want you and you," I say pointing to two of the girls, "to get out on the dance floor right now." The girls look at each other, giggle, and comply.

"How'd you like to go for a drive later?" I say to the girl I am paired with.

"Where to?"

"Where to doesn't matter." I lean close. "The only thing that counts is 'what' we do." The girl backs away.

"I'm sorry, but I'm supposed to stay with my friends."

"Then go back to your friends," I snarl and stalk off the floor. After the number ends, Matt joins me along the side.

"What's wrong with you?" he asks for the second time. "If you keep dumping girls, we'll run out before the night's over."

"A dime a dozen," I mutter. I survey the room. "Over there," I point toward two girls wearing heavy makeup and loud clothes. "The jackpot."

"I don't know . . ." Matt begins as I start off. Reluctantly, he follows.

"Hello there, beautiful," I address one of the girls. Her mascaraed eyes widen in surprise. "What's your name?"

"Marsha Henderson," she replies. "What's yours, good-looking?"

"Dudding," I reply without hesitation. "Bob Dudding."

"Where you from?" She coos.

"Outer space. Where else?"

"Oooh, that's cool," Marsha squeals. "Where in outer space?"

"The planet Zanzador."

"What are you doing here on earth?"

I lower my voice. "My mission," I begin, "is to find the cutest girl on planet earth, kidnap her, and bring her back to my galaxy."

"Oooh," she grabs my arm in excitement. "But how do I know for sure you're really from outer space?"

I drop my voice even lower. "Persons from the planet Zanzador are marked with a secret code. This code has never before been revealed to earthlings. But since I am going to take you away, I'll make an exception." I grab her hand and lead her over to a black light. I place my left hand under the ultraviolet rays.

"Admit one." The words glow in eerie purple.

"Ooooh, take me, I'm yours."

CHAPTER 5

The Blue Beast retraces the route to the clearing in the woods. Matt drives with one arm around the girl who calls herself Elaine. I embrace Marsha.

Maneuvering the Blue Beast into the clearing, Matt coasts to a stop. "We're going for a walk," he informs Marsha and me. "You guys have fun and don't do anything we wouldn't do." He flashes a grin. They get out and disappear through the brush into the night. I turn my attention to Marsha. She repels my advances, gently pushing me away.

"Hey, we hardly know each other." Her tone of voice suggests that she wants to hear my life story.

"I told you I'm from Zanzador," I kid, hoping to prolong the charade. "And you're under my control." I attempt to pull her close. She gives me a maternal smile and shrugs off the embrace.

"No, really," she continues. "You seem like a nice guy. I'd like to know more about you."

I feel cheated. Nice guy, I sulk. Do you think I brought you all the way out here because I'm a nice guy and I want to tell you all about my past. If I was looking for someone to bring home to Mom, I would have found someone better than you at the dance. In fact, I wouldn't even be looking there.

My mind races. Hypocrite! I accuse myself. I have a lot of nerve making that kind of judgment. After all, look what was on my mind.

My head begins to spin. The pungent night air and the sickening sweet smell of her strong perfume overcome me. The effects of the booze combine with my growing feelings of guilt and, suddenly, I feel queasy.

A knot forms in my stomach and rapidly expands. I jump out of the car and sprint across the clearing into the bushes. Dizzily I lean one shoulder against a tree and vomit. When there is nothing more to puke, I begin to retch dry, foul air. The ground begins to spin, faster and faster, like a Ferris wheel gone berserk. The tree I clutch has become the unsteady hub of this whirling chaos. I grasp it tightly, struggling to stay on my feet.

"Dear God, oh dear God," I murmer over and over. I feel alone and deserted. Tears well up in my eyes. Sobs heave in my chest and soon I'm bawling like a baby.

"Get a grip on yourself, get a grip on yourself," I repeat to myself. The sobs finally subside and the carrousel grinds to a stop. I stumble back to the car.

I find Marsha still sitting in the backseat. I open the door, plop down beside her, lean back, and close my eyes. Marsha scoots over to me and takes my hand in hers.

"You okay?" she asks. I feel her dab the tears from my cheeks with a hanky. Even that reeks of cheap perfume.

"Yeah, I'll live," I mutter.

"Is it my fault?" she asks somberly.

"No, no, I'm just not used to . . . ." My voice trails off.

"Do you feel like talking?"

"I don't care." I hope she can tell by the tone of my

voice that I don't want to. She doesn't take the hint.

"Where are you from?" She sits forward and looks at me. I try to puncture her compassion with surliness. "What difference does it make?"

"I just want to know. Please tell me." She tilts her head in an awkward attempt at looking demure.

I turn and look closely at Marsha for the first time. She is not pretty. Her features are oversized. Her face is puffy and slightly oily. I decide to answer her questions, but not to do anything that will encourage her to think I like her. My first impulse is to lie to her about where I live, but I'm tired of lying.

"Spireville," I mumble in a barely audible voice.

"Where?"

"Spireville."

"Is that here in Indiana?"

"Naw, Illinois."

"Illinois!" Her eyes light up. "I'm from Illinois!" She waits for me to ask the obvious question.

"Oh, yeah? Where in Illinois?" I ask dutifully.

"Peoria." I gulp. She continues: "Is Spireville anywhere close to Peoria?"

Dumb broad, I think to myself. How can you live in Peoria and not know that Spireville is only twenty miles away.

"I don't know," I fib. "Coupla hours, maybe."

She's crestfallen. "Oh. Well, maybe sometime we'll get lucky and our paths will cross again."

Mercifully, Matt and Elaine emerge from the shadows and rejoin us. From the way they act, and the way Matt's hair is mussed, they seem to have had a good time.

Looking in the window, Matt asks, "How did you two make out?" I glare at him as I get out of the car and stretch.

I glance at my watch. "Hey," I exclaim, trying to sound alarmed. "Look what time it is! We'd better be getting back or the others will really be ticked."

"So soon?" Elaine grumbles.

"I'll tell you what," I volunteer. "I'll drive and you two can have the backseat."

"Okay, but take it slow," Matt orders. He and Elaine crowd together. Marsha moves to the front. She slides next to me and lays her head on my shoulder. I start the car and spin out of the clearing. I floor the accelerator all the way back to the resort.

We drop the girls off at their cabin. Matt walks Elaine to the door for a long good-bye kiss. I remain planted behind the wheel. Marsha is silent for a while. Finally she speaks.

"This has been a special night for me. I feel we really got close." I try to respond but the words stick in my throat. She holds up the handkerchief she has been clutching in her hand. "I'm going to keep this hanky as a souvenir." I nod my head silently.

Matt approaches the car. "Well, good-bye," Marsha whispers.

"G-G-Good-bye," I stammer. She leans over and kisses me on the cheek. I shut my eyes tightly as she gets out of the car and walks to the door.

"Hey," Matt exclaims as we drive back to the boardwalk. "Did you know they're from Peoria?" Maybe you and I can go up and see them sometime." I shoot Matt another withering glare. He gets the message this time and breaks out into laughter.

Steve, Chuck, Allen, and Denny are waiting for us when we arrive at the boardwalk. They pile in, all jabbering at the same time.

"Where to?" I ask.

"I'm starved," Chuck says. "Find some place to eat."

"At midnight?"

"There's gotta be something open." I begin to cruise around. Denny and Allen pick up an argument that sounds as if it has been running for some time.

"Don't blame me," Denny says hotly. "Every time you picked out the girls, they said they were already with somebody else."

"Well, I wasn't about to get hooked up with the dogs you were after," Allen retorts. "I'd rather have nothing than some of those woofers."

"Yeah, well that's what we ended up with—nothing."

"We wouldn't have if you hadn't blown our big chance."

"Whaddya mean by that?"

"You know what I mean," Allen shoots back. "Those two cute blondes. They were coming along. If you hadn't tried to convince them that you knew karate... ."

"Oh, yeah, and you wearing your glasses upside down really helped."

"At least I didn't tell them the rip in my pants was a gunshot wound." The rest of us laugh. Allen and Denny fall into sullen silence.

"How about you guys?" Steve asks. "How did you do?" I interupt Matt as he begins to answer.

"How about you?" I return the question. "Why don't you say how you did for a change?"

"I would but I don't want to embarrass any virgin ears," Steve leers.

"Struck out, huh?" I retort abruptly. I can't see Steve's face but I can sense that my reply has angered him.

"Springer, the things I do you only dream about," he snaps.

"Hey, you just passed a place to eat," Chuck yells. I whip a U-turn and pull the car to a stop in a crowded parking lot.

To our surprise, we find the restaurant deserted. The building is partitioned into two parts, and evidently the people are on the other side. From the strains of country-Western music filtering through the partition, we guess that the other side is some sort of nightclub.

Steve walks behind the counter and helps himself to a glass of water. Denny investigates the room. "It says here to ring this bell for service," he calls over to the rest of us.

"Well, ring it then," Steve says.

"Yeah, try to do something right for once," Allen snaps. Denny rings the bell and a few moments later a waitress appears. "Whaddya want," she rasps. We give our orders and she disappears. While waiting for our food, we keep ourselves occupied by holding our version of the coffee shop olympics.

Allen wins the first event which calls for balancing a salt shaker on edge. Steve becomes the first to flip a fork into a glass of water. Matt takes the distance prize for shooting paper wads with straws; I win for accuracy. We are in the middle of the highly competitive sticking-butter-patties-on-the-ceiling-by-flipping-them-with-a-knife event when the food arrives. The waitress unceremoniously dumps our orders in front of us and disappears.

"These waitresses, always bucking for a tip," Steve remarks sarcastically. We straighten out the order so the right food is in front of the right person. The food is greasy and undercooked but satisfies our hungry stomachs. Chuck leans back and emits a tremendous belch. The rest join in the competition, but Chuck is declared the grossest of our lot by unanimous decision.

"Well, tomorrow it's home-sweet-home," Denny begins.

"Yes, and work-sour-work," Allen adds.

"At least we have two days to rest up first," says Matt.

Chuck yawns. "Yeah, and I'm gonna sleep for two days solid."

Allen asks, "You guys have your detasseling crews lined up yet?" We all nod yes with the exception of Steve who says he has one more spot to fill.

"Hey, Jon," Allen remarks. "I hear you've got Donna Timmons on your crew."

Steve's fork clatters to the floor and he straightens up. "Are you kidding? Is that true?"

"You heard the man," I reply. I can see that Steve is surprised. Donna is the cutest girl in Spireville. She moved into the area less than a year ago and has been the center of attention for most of the guys ever since. Steve had dated Donna most of the year and everyone assumed they were going together. But, the last few weeks of school Donna had begun acting friendly toward me. I gave her several lifts home from school and on one occasion had mustered the courage to ask her to be on my crew. I wasn't surprised that Steve hadn't asked her for his crew yet since he has a way of taking things for granted. But, I was surprised when she said yes.

Steve pursues the matter. "You knew I was saving a spot on my crew for her."

"First come, first served," I reply.

"Well, I say it's a rotten deal," Steve mutters.

Matt intervenes. "Look, Steve, Jon just beat you to the punch. He took you fair and square."

Steve leans back. His eyes narrow slightly. "Well, it's not who has her first, it's who has her last that counts."

58

"What's that supposed to mean?" I demand. Steve doesn't reply. We fall silent, toying with our silverware and cups. The elements of the night are overcoming us and we're beginning to feel weary.

"Where's that waitress?" Chuck wonders aloud. "I'd like to get out of here. Denny, go ring that bell." Denny does and we wait a while longer.

After a few minutes with no response, Chuck gets up and rings the bell ferociously. We wait, but still no waitress. The music from the other side of the partition blares on.

"Listen," Steve suggests, "I say if they don't want our money, let's just take off." An argument breaks out with three for Steve's suggestion and three against. But after another ringing of the bell and more waiting the vote is unanimous.

"Okay," Steve says, "on the count of ten we all head for the side door. When we get to the car, jump in and you, Jon, drive like it's the Indy 500." Steve counts to ten. We hold our breath in nervous anticipation. On eight we slowly slide our chairs back. On ten we race for the door. Steve hits it first.

Clang-g-g-g-g!

"Oh, no, an alarm, Steve hisses. "Run for it." We're almost to the car when Matt stops in his tracks.

"Hey, my jacket! I left it on my chair."

"Forget your jacket. It won't do you any good in jail."

"But, my billfold's in it!" Matt pivots and sprints back to the restaurant. The rest of us crawl all over each other getting into the car.

"Get this heap going," Steve commands.

"What about Matt?"

"We'll come back for him later." My hand shakes as I

59

fumble to insert the key into the ignition. After several tries, the engine turns over and roars to life.

By now people are pouring out of the club. "There they go," I hear a voice scream as I turn onto the street.

Twe-e-e-et!

"Police. Stop or I'll shoot!" a voice booms.

"Floor it. He's bluffing," Steve urges. I jam on the brakes and pull back into the parking lot.

The night guard waits until we all get out of the car before he holsters his gun. "You boys are lucky you stopped. If you'd kept going, you'd have had a few bullet holes in the side of your car to explain to your folks."

A heavyset man who appears to be the manager walks up alongside the guard. Patrons from the club press around tightly, drinks still in hand. The guard addresses the large man. "Well, what should we do with them, Bud?"

Bud eyes us silently, a toothpick clenched between his teeth. His patrons are not so quiet.

"Throw 'em in the can," a husky voice calls from the rear. Others chorus their approval.

"But, we were going to pay," Allen says in protest. "Only we couldn't . . . ." His voice is drowned out in the shouts of the crowd.

"I say string 'em up!" shrieks a scrawny, red-haired woman. The crowd erupts in laughter.

I strain my neck and spot Matt standing in the middle of the crowd grinning impishly. The waitress spots him too.

"That guy there," she points at Matt. "He was with them too."

The grin on Matt's face disappears. Arms shove him roughly in our direction. Like Peter, he can't deny his past.

60

"Well, Bud, what'll it be?" the guard repeats.

"Have them pay what they owe and let 'em go," Bud replies in a low, even voice. The crowd boos this suggestion.

The guard takes off his hat and scratches his head. "Well, if that's the way you want it . . . "

The waitress breaks in, "I say they pay double what they owe." The crowd applauds.

"You tell 'em, Agnes," someone shouts. Bud nods his head, turns away, and heads back toward the club. The crowd gradually breaks up and follows him back inside. We settle up with Agnes and depart.

Back in the car, Steve is disgusted. "We could've made it if Jon hadn't chickened out."

"Sure," Denny says, "we'd have made it with bullet holes in the car and maybe our heads."

"Well," Chuck sighs, "we can thank our lucky stars they didn't lock us up."

"That's no lie," Allen echoes. "Let's get back to the cabin—before something else happens!"

"After we do one more thing," Steve says. Everyone groans.

"I'm heading back," I say firmly.

"Go ahead," Steve replies. "I need something from the cabin anyhow."

I park in front of the cabin and start to get out. Steve immediately dashes inside and returns before any of us have gotten very far. "C'mon, let's go," he orders.

"Not me," I say. "I'm hitting the sack."

"Go ahead," Steve replies. "The rest of you are coming, aren't you?" Silence.

"How long will it take?" Chuck asks.

"Not long, not long at all." I survey the others. They

have resigned themselves to going along. I mutter, get back in, and slam my door closed.

"Where to?"

"Just head out the same way we came in last Sunday." As I drive, a foul odor reaches my nose. I adjust my mirror and see the dim outline of a heavy glass jar on Steve's lap.

"What in the world are you going to do with those cockroaches?" I ask.

"You just do the driving, okay?" I try to ignore the smell but it reeks of death and decay.

"The least you can do is hold the stinking thing out the window."

"In a minute, in a minute." Steve is engrossed in tying a faded red ribbon that he found in the cabin around the middle of the jar. He finishes and complies with my suggestion.

"Slow down," Steve orders. "Slow down." I ease my foot off the accelerator. "There, pull off to the left." I turn off the highway and pull to a stop. I look around in bewilderment. Everything is dark except for a solitary neon sign. I lean out the window and squint up at it.

"Woody's Cafe," it glows.

Suddenly I understand. Steve has already left the car and is standing next to the large picture window at the front of the restaurant. I can barely make out his form in the eerie illumination of the sign. I strain my eyes and see his body coil. One arm draws back.

Crash! Tinkle, tinkle.

CHAPTER 6

I am trapped alone in a small room with walls of rotted wood. The room is dark but I can smell the stench of garbage strewn about. I hear a click and suddenly I'm blinded by the intense beam from a naked light bulb hanging overhead. When my eyes clear and focus, I see a heavy jar full of horrible, swarming black bugs sitting on the shelf. Their claws scrape at the glass and my ears can pick up their high-pitched screeching.

While I watch, the rotted shelf buckles and the jar begins to teeter. I try to run and grab the jar before it falls, but my feet are frozen to the floor. The jar crashes, shattering into a thousand pieces. Throngs of black creatures spill onto the floor. At first they mill about in confusion, but then they organize and begin to march — straight toward me.

In the glare of the light, I can see their tiny fangs gnashing. I know that they have been without food for days. I grab for the hanging light, hoping its intensity will fend them off. The light explodes at my touch. I cry out in pain as splinters of glass tear into my hands.

In the darkness, I hear the ominous scratching of legions of tiny legs marching across the dry wood floorboards. I back up until I am against the wall. The roaches sweep toward me in waves. They swirl angrily about my feet. I panic and begin to run. I trip and land with a sickening scrunch on thousands of their small bodies.

Now the cockroaches swarm over me. They infest my clothes and hair. I swat at them but every blow brings more of the vengeful creatures down upon me. I scream in agony.

A dimly lit face appears in the window. I cry for help. The face presses spookily against the glass. It's the hollowed-out face of an old man.

The jaws gape. "I told you to be a good boy. I warned you not to get in any trouble."

"Please help me," I beg. "I won't do it again."

"Too late now," the voice moans. "I told you to be a good boy. I warned you not to get in trouble."

The face vanishes. I feel my strength give way. My body is rapidly being covered by the miniature vampires —when a pleasant voice sings out. "Breakfast, Jon. Break-fast."

I sit up and look around. I see my pump-handle lamp, a familiar chest of drawers. . . .

"Coming, Mom," I yell. I crawl out from under twisted covers and dress.

In the dining room I glance at the clock. Eight-thirty. "Where's everybody at?" I ask, pulling a chair to the table.

"Martha and David already left for work," Mom calls from the kitchen. "Dad had some errands to do, so he took off too. The two youngsters are still sleeping." I make a mental note that someday I'll have to find out what a pastor does with all his time.

"I've got to be on my way in fifteen minutes," I say much louder than I need to since the kitchen adjoins the dining room. The remark is meant to hurry Mom up with the food.

"Now that you've had your big fling, you'll have to start getting up at a decent time again," Mom replies cheerfully. This is one of the few references that either Mom or Dad has made to Indiana Beach. I figure they decided to use the "coals of fire" strategy on me.

"You're just lucky you have this job," Mom continues. "For most jobs you'd have to be at work earlier than this."

"Fields are too wet this time of year," I remark with the authority of an expert. "Soon there won't be so much dew and then I'll be gone before the rest of you even wake up."

Mom laughs. "That'll be the day." A few seconds later she appears with a platter full of scrambled eggs, toast, and bacon.

"Why all the food?" I inquire. "I'm the only one eating."

"Oh, I haven't eaten yet, and you'll need a full stomach if you're going to do a hard day's work."

"I'm not planning to do a hard day's work. I'm just planning to sit in the seat and guide that machine down the rows," I joke. "Might even take a nap now and then."

"Well, you'd better eat anyway." Mom sets the food in front of me and then places two unopened envelopes against my glass of juice.

"What's this?"

"Look for yourself," Mom says, beaming. I tear open the envelopes and confirm my guess that they are acceptance letters from the two colleges where I've applied. I sent applications to Southern, a state school in Illinois where the rest of the gang applied, and Creston, a

Mennonite college in Kansas which only Matt and I tried.

Mom hovers over me. "They came while you were gone. A man from Creston called and said if you go there you'd qualify for a grant."

"That's big of them, since Creston's so expensive to start with."

"Jon, you know it's not a question of money. We're not rich, but with the grant, your father and I could help you make it." I detect a note of fear that I might not choose the church college. I set the letters aside and begin to eat.

Mom hardly waits for me to swallow. "Well?"

"Well, what?"

"Well, have you decided which one you're going to accept?"

"I don't know. I'll think about it for a while — talk to the other guys . . . ."

Mom gets to her feet. "Jon, you can't always do things just because everybody else does. You've got to start making your own decisions."

"Then how's come I get the feeling that you're trying to make us choose Creston?" I reply.

"Well . . . . Why not? Creston's a good school."

"What makes it better than any other college?"

"It's Christian for one thing. Your brother Luke might not be in Voluntary Service in Wichita now if he hadn't gone to a church college. Some of his Mennonite classmates who went to state universities joined the army when they got drafted."

"I'll think it over," I say with finality.

We eat for a few minutes in silence.

"By the way," Mom begins. This is her way of introducing a subject out of the blue as if it were the next logical step in a conversation. "I was surprised to hear you hadn't asked Sharon Litwiller to be on your crew."

"There's only six to a crew. I couldn't ask everybody."

"But you and Sharon always got along so well."

"Well, I can't have everybody on my crew—just because I get along with them."

"I know. It's just that you and Sharon seem like such a good couple . . . ."

"Maybe that's why I didn't ask her. Just because we're friends, everybody's expecting us to get married or something."

I gulp a final mouthful of food. "I'd better go or I'll be late." I push back my chair and start for the door. Mom hurries to get my lunch bucket from the refrigerator. I wave good-bye as I run out the door. I back our secondhand Plymouth out of the garage and honk as I head down the road.

My first stop is to pick up Donna Timmons. I have painstakingly planned my route for picking up my six crew members. The plan has nothing to do with saving gas.

I figure we'll need to sit three to the front and four in the back. Donna is first so she'll naturally sit in the front. The next three will logically sit in the back. Then the sixth person will have to sit in front, resulting in Donna being squeezed up against me as I maneuver the Plymouth with its three-on-the-tree transmission down the road. I've gone over this pleasant scenario a dozen times in my mind.

I ease the car carefully into the circular drive in front of the Timmons' vine-covered brick house. By the time I pull to a stop at the sidewalk, Donna is on the porch saying good-bye to her mother. Framed on either side by rose trellises, she looks as if she is just stepping off the fashion pages of a Sears catalog. She's wearing denim jeans with a matching jacket, brightly set off by a red and white checkered shirt. Her thick, brunette hair is neatly wrapped in a blue bandana. Sunglasses hide her large, warm brown eyes, but I guess they are accented with the same light makeup that gives her cheeks their rosy look. I declare to myself that I just may be in love—sort of, anyhow.

I give my own carefully chosen apparel a final once-over. Worn sneakers, neatly patched jeans, a T-shirt over which I am wearing a long-sleeved plaid shirt—all carefully calculated to give me a he-man look. My sleeves are rolled up to my elbows to reinforce the masculine image and accent the sterling silver of my watchband and the white gold of my class ring.

My souvenir hat from Indiana Beach provides the final touch. For a time I debated whether to wear the hat—but finally came out in favor of it for two reasons. It would provide a natural opening for conversation with Donna, and it would keep my fly-away wisps of hair in check during the course of the day.

After hugging her Mom and waving good-bye to her little brother, Donna skips to the car. In following the graceful flow of her form, I almost forget to reach over and open the door. She sets her lunch on the floor and glides in beside me. "Hello, Jon," she chirps. I nod somberly.

Too somberly, I correct myself as we get underway. Don't overdo the masculine bit. I mull over how to introduce the subject of Indiana Beach. Donna beats me to the punch.

"I hear you guys had a great time at Indiana Beach!"

If she had asked that as a question, I'd have had all kinds of replies. Put so matter-of-factly, her statement leaves me almost speechless.

"Uh, yes, how did you know?"

"Oh, Steve stopped by awhile last night and told me all about it." I grit my teeth. So that was why Steve didn't get together with the rest of the gang yesterday.

"*All* about it?" I ask.

Donna smiles coyly. "Well, not everything, of course."

I thrust my shoulders back. "Yeah, we had a pretty good time out there." I feel on top of things again.

While we're waiting for our second passenger to come out, I make a daring move. I take her hand from its resting place on the seat and turn it palm-up. "Have you been soaking your hands in salt water like I told you to?" This is the recommended practice for detasselers to toughen their hands.

Donna smiles impishly. "No, I wanted to keep them just as soft and feminine as I could." My heartbeat increases two decibels.

I clear my throat and speak with a note of concern. "That's all well and good except for the fact that the leaves on cornstalks cut soft hands to shreds."

"But we can wear gloves, can't we? I brought some along." Donna holds up a pair of thick rubber gloves.

"You can, but your hands get so hot most people end up taking them off. Also, you break more tassels when you're wearing gloves. But don't worry," I reassure her. "Someone as tough as you shouldn't have any problems." I pat her on the shoulder, grateful to have another excuse for contact.

I pick up my remaining passengers and head for the rendezvous at the Frontier Seed Corn Company. I pull into the parking lot. My crew piles out of the car and heads to where their fellow crew members are grouped together. I head for the 15-or-so drivers who stand off to one side. Steve spots Donna and whistles at her. I see, to my chagrin, that she returns a wave and flirtatious smile.

Clang! Clang! The burly foreman bangs a pipe wrench against the chassis of an old detasseling machine to call us to order.

"Okay, crews and drivers, over this way," he hollers. After most of the workers have gathered around, the foreman begins explaining the finer points of detasseling. We crew drivers—veterans who have worked our way up through the ranks—stand to the side looking properly bored with this speech geared for the novices.

The foreman first makes an attempt to explain the process of hybridization. "When you cross-pollinate one kind of corn with another, you get a hybrid, right?" The 80-odd detasselers nod in mute agreement. "Okay, now what we'll be working with is called a double hybrid. What I'm calling the male corn has been produced by cross-pollinating type A with type B. The female corn has been produced by crossing type C with type D. Got that? Okay, now what we want to do in these fields is cross the pollen of male corn A and B with the ears of female corn C and D." He pauses. "Any questions so far?" There aren't any.

Now the foreman gets to the nitty-gritty. "Okay, the corn is planted twelve rows female, two rows male, twelve rows female and so on. You pull the tassels on the female corn *only*," he emphasizes. I prepare myself for his standard off-color joke. "Try pulling the tassel on a male stalk of corn and it might pull right back."

The foreman concludes his lecture. "Now remember, you get all of the tassels and all of each tassel. If you just get part of a tassel, it will grow right back and pollinate. That might not seem serious, but there are millions of

70

grains of pollen on each tassel. Okay, last chance for questions." There still aren't any.

I tense for the next part of the ritual—the choosing of machines. This luxury is left to the crew bosses. While acting nonchalant, we have been eyeing the detasseling machines lined up in the background. The spindly machines look like an invading army of giant spiders carrying baskets for storing loot. The baskets are where the crew will stand for the torturous task of stripping the female corn of its tassels. By now I know that each of us has picked a machine. With apprehension, I realize that more than one of us will be after the same machine this year—the bright red one. Although the machine is brand new, my main reason for choosing it is that red is Donna's favorite color—a fact she has well publicized.

We begin to edge toward the machines which are parked 50 yards away. "Okay," the foreman concludes, "if there are no questions, crew leaders . . . *pick your machines!*" We bolt for the rigs, our crews cheering us loudly. The three of us head for the bright red machine. We race neck and neck. Allen is in the middle, I'm on the right, Steve is on the left.

Twenty yards from the machine I resort to underhanded tactics. I nudge Allen into Steve's path. The ploy works perfectly. Allen stumbles in front of Steve. The two collide and tumble into the dirt. By the time they get back to their feet, I am straddling the driver's seat of the bright red rig, and all the other drivers have claimed their machines. Steve's face is a mask of rage. He mouths a word to me which I don't need to hear to understand.

I shrug. "All's fair in love and war."

"You said it," Steve growls. "All's fair." Allen and he have to settle for the two remaining machines, a sickly orange one and one from which time has erased all color. We wave to our crews and they rush to join us. The foreman strides up and down the line of machines, giving last-minute instructions to the drivers. Then he stands back, pulls a red hanky from his back pocket, and waves for us to start our engines.

Up and down the line two-cylinder engines sputter and roar. Allen's clunker proves to be stubborn and it takes five minutes of tinkering to get results. Finally, all of the machines are putt-putting away. The foreman raises his hanky and drops it. With that signal, we grind our machines into gear and roll off toward our destinations at the top speed of five miles per hour.

The gentle morning sun rises small and warm in the clear Illinois sky. From my comfortable perch, I feel sorry for those who must stand in the baskets and do the dirty work. I don't feel too much sympathy, however, because I remember the hours I spent there myself the last three summers. I can still feel the dew and sweat that soaks your clothing in the morning, then turns sticky and itchy in the midday heat. I remember the endless waves of stalks that pass by hypnotically at eye level. And I can recall all too well the back strain and heaviness of arms that result from tugging countless reluctant tassels from their fibrous wombs. I wince at the memory of the ragged leaves that tear and claw at unprotected skin. And finally, I think of the insult added to injury when a tassel breaks and you're sent back to fight your way through a row for the offender—while everyone else takes a breather.

My crew survives the morning in spite or because of constant griping. For dinner, I join the drivers who sprawl under a huge maple, wolfing down sandwiches and gulping the lemonade provided for us. Traditionally the drivers do not eat with their crews. The reason given is that each group has a different part of their anatomy to complain about.

"Hey, Allen," Denny manages between mouthfuls. "Your crew is missing so many tassels that I can't tell where you've been and where you haven't."

"Yeah, well just tell your crew to pull tassels with their hands and not with their feet."

"At least I can keep my machine in the row. I saw you knock down ten feet of corn."

"I can't help that. Something's wrong with the steering on my old clunker." That brings some jeers. "Hey Jon," Chuck says with a wink. "I'll bet you like sitting up there where you can look right down ol' Donna's blouse!" The others grin, so I smile knowingly. Actually the thought hadn't occurred to me.

We finish dinner and stretch out in the shade for catnaps.

A toot from the foreman's pickup signals the end of our siesta. We smear ourselves with suntan lotion and head back to our machines.

To make the afternoon pass more quickly, I play a nonpacifistic game in my mind. I pretend I'm carrying a load of ammo through a highly sensitive mine field. One brush against either side and—ka-boom! I guide my specially designed, high-speed apparatus back and forth through the forbidding maze.

The distant blast of a horn marks the end of the workday. I head back toward the seed corn company and park my machine in its place. Everyone is too tired to be sociable. We pile into our cars and drive off in different directions.

I quickly drop off the others with a half-hearty, "See ya

tomorrow." Then I cruise more slowly toward the Timmons place. Donna looks like a ball of yarn come unraveled. Strands of hair hang down over her face. Her shirttail sticks out and her makeup is streaked and blotted by sweat. She rubs her hands together and I can see she's in pain.

"You were right," she moans. "Gloves don't work too well." She holds her mutilated hands up for me to see.

"It's too late for salt water now," I sympathize. "You'll have to tough it out."

"Yeah, guess I should have listened to you." She smiles ruefully. "Do you have any suggestions now?"

"Well, one," I suggest slyly.

"What's that?"

"A relaxing evening with a refined gentleman."

"And just how will that help my hands?"

"Oh, it won't, but it'll help take your mind off them." She breaks into musical laughter.

We arrive at Donna's house too quickly. I swing into her drive and coast to a stop. Donna jumps out and bounces around to my open window. She leans close. "I'm going to try rubbing these hands with salve, but if that doesn't work I may just give you a call." She winks, turns, and runs up the walk.

I watch until she disappears into the house, then float home on a cushion of air.

CHAPTER 7

"Springer, come here a minute. I wanna talk with you!"
The burly foreman's voice booms for miles. It is Saturday,
the last day of the first week of the detasseling season. My
crew meanders toward our machine, watching over their
shoulders. I hurry over to the foreman. He waits for me to
speak first.

"What do you want?" I ask.

"How much are we paying you?"

"Three-fifty an hour." I have a sinking feeling that this
isn't to be a social chat.

"Why do you think we pay you that money?"

I try to answer this loaded question without sounding
smart-alecky. "To drive the machine, I guess."

The foreman increases his volume. "It's not just to drive
the machine. A trained chimpanzee could steer one of
those contraptions. We pay you to keep an eye on your
crew. What were you doing out there yesterday? Taking a
nap? I checked your rows and found more broken tassels
than you could shake a stick at." He pauses as if I'm
supposed to respond.

"I'm sorry. I'll try to do better," I reply feebly.

"You'd better do more than try. We got a stack of

applications for crew boss as high as your head from people who would love to have your machine." He turns and stalks away. If the foreman was trying to humiliate me, he did a good job. Nobody could have missed that lecture—even if they'd wanted to.

I try to compose myself, then stroll back to my machine with as much dignity as I can muster. Steve grins down at me from his perch, letting me know he didn't miss a word. As I pass by Denny, he jumps off his machine and falls into stride with me.

"Don't let ol' George get to you, Jon. Dad says he's all bark and no bite." Around us, rigs begin to start up. Denny stops and turns to go back to his rig. "Hey," he calls after me.

I stop. "What?"

"We missed you last night. Where were you?"

"Uh, I was over at Donna's."

"Again? You're going to turn into a married man." Denny moves closer and says confidentially, "You should have been with us last night."

"Why?"

"Jack Griffin got us some hooch." I have to think a moment before I realize what he's talking about.

"Oh yeah, how much?" I ask, feigning interest.

"Tell you all about it at lunch. We'd better get going." Denny wheels and sprints back to his machine.

The late June sun beats harshly down from a barren sky casting stark, diagonal shadows on the rows of corn. I have replaced my Indiana Beach hat with a more functional straw one. My crew is composed of four tanners and two burners. The tanners are stripped to the bare necessities of clothing—cut-offs for the guys and bathing suits for the girls. The burners are comically bundled up in caps and long-sleeved clothing more appropriate for an October chill than a June roast.

If I've been missing broken tassels it may have something to do with Donna. Now, with her sun-lightened hair, a deep bronze tan, and her white, close-fitting bathing suit, I have hardly been able to keep my eyes off her.

Since Monday I have been with Donna four out of five nights. I'd be on top of the world except for one thing—I can't shake the suspicion that Donna is using me to make Steve jealous. The signs are small ones but they're there—like the way she looks over at him when we pass his crew in the field, or the way she reacts when I happen to mention his name. My relationship with Donna is not the only thing bothering me. In fact, of my current worries, it doesn't even top the list.

We're giving a field its second combing this morning. Most of the tassels are pulled on the first round so the extent of my supervision will consist of a backward glance every thirty seconds or so and a reprimand every ten minutes to keep the younger members of my crew from goofing off. I bark at Fred, the youngest crew member, for performing gymnastics on the railing around his basket.

I come to the end of a row, turn the machine around, and head back up the field. My mind races over the several topics that need thought and selects an order. I give first priority to the gang. This week, since I began seeing Donna, I haven't spent much time with the gang. The one time I was with them I couldn't help feeling that we were growing apart. Something indefinable seems to have happened to the group at Indiana Beach—like we all passed through some sort of giant machine, each coming out different.

The subject of church is one indicator of the change in the group. In the past much of our conversation centered around issues, events, and persons related to church, Sunday school, and youth group. Each time someone mentions the church now, however, the conversation becomes stifled. After an awkward silence someone changes the subject.

Another thing that concerns me is the drinking the gang has begun doing. Twice this week the others have gotten hold of some beer and gone drinking—three times counting last night. Maybe I'm naive but I thought our bender at Indiana Beach was a one-time fling, "the cold, dark waters of evil" to test and then withdraw from. Apparently the rest didn't feel the same—although both Allen and Matt confessed that the drinking bothered them. Matt told me that the second time, after drinking in the country, they came back into town and played a reckless game of "ditch-em" with their cars. He was sure that Spireville's lone cop knew what was happening but choose to ignore it for the time being.

What concerns me as much as the drinking is the pranks the gang's been pulling. I *was* in on this. Coach Dudding has become the prime target of our mischief. The coach runs a small farm a mile from town. The night I went out with the gang we had decided to get even with him for the last day of school. All we had planned to do was blow up some beehives with cherry bombs or set his truck up on blocks. But, one thing led to another and we ended up pouring sand into the radiator of his old Ford tractor. I heard that he was going to have to junk it and buy a new one.

We stop at the end of the field for a midmorning water break. After drinking our fill, we empty our bottles with a water fight. This is the kind of conflict the world needs more of, I think. You vent your hostilities and everyone ends up refreshed.

Back in the field, my thoughts turn to my own impending conflict. My birthday is coming up next week. Usually that would be something to celebrate. But this, being my eighteenth, means that I'll have to register for the draft. And, as yet, I haven't decided whether to go 1-0 or 1-A. How can I make such an important decision in so short a time? How can the government expect anyone to make such a big decision at so young an age? Of course, as far as the government's concerned, there shouldn't have to be a choice. Everyone should go into the military. Maybe that's why they make you decide so young. They're afraid if you think about it you won't serve.

But why not serve? We have a good country. If someone is evil enough to try to take it away from us, shouldn't we stand up for our rights and fight them? Yes, but in recent wars it's been our country going over and fighting in other countries. Even if I would fight to defend my country, I shouldn't fight in an army that takes over other people's countries. My mind bogs down from this line of reasoning and I take a new tack.

I think of the sermons and lectures I've heard on peace. Jesus certainly seemed to believe in peace. He said, "Blessed are the peacemakers, for they shall be called sons of God." I've never had the urge to kill anything more than a rabbit during hunting season. So shouldn't I just go 1-0?

But the counterarguments flood back. Jesus drove the money changers out of the temple with force. Samuel, in the Old Testament, hacked a king to death on orders from God. So shouldn't a Christian nation use force to fight evil in the world? Anyway, isn't killing a relative thing? If a thousand people could be saved by killing one person, wouldn't I do it? If by stopping the communists, large-scale massacres can be prevented, isn't that the thing to do?

If the picture isn't confused enough already, I add the evidence of my own behavior to it. The escapades at Indiana Beach flash through my mind. I think of the pranks on Dudding. Blowing up beehives is hardly a witness of peace. If I were really a peacemaker, wouldn't I be handling these situations differently?

I try to wash away my confusion with a flood of self-pity. If only I wasn't Mennonite, I wouldn't be faced with such questions. I would be free from this yoke that now crushes down upon me. My eyes blur in salty anger. Sometimes I think it was easier to be crucified on a cross than to grow up Mennonite on the cornfield plains of Illinois!

"Hey, watch out!"

The machine has veered and is mowing down six rows of corn simultaneously. I swerve back on course, throwing my crew off balance. I jam in the clutch and come to a halt. Members of my crew get back up and brush themselves off. I look back over my shoulder at thirty feet of flattened foliage. My stomach turns a flip-flop.

Donna squints up at me. "Are you okay?"

I shake my head lamely. "I won't be if the foreman sees this."

At lunch, the rest of the gang is as boisterous as I am sullen. They brag openly about their drinking—each person claiming to have drunk the most and to have acted the soberest. Their revelry drifts in and out of my consciousness. I nibble at my food, lost in my thoughts.

Halfway through dinner I nudge Matt. "Hey, can we go

over there and talk a little?" Steve overhears the comment.

"What's the matter? You got something to say that the rest of us can't hear?"

"No, it's not that. I just didn't think you'd be interested."

"Now what could be bothering you that your ol' gang wouldn't want to be in on?" As usual Steve's question is doubled-edged.

"Yeah, come on, Jon. What is it?" Allen speaks more sincerely.

"Well . . ." I hesitate, "it's just that I've got to register next week sometime and I'm still not sure what status to ask for on my classification questionnaire."

"You were right," Steve says. "We're not interested."

"You'd better be interested," Matt replies. "It affects you too."

"Okay, then, I'll be interested." Turning to me, Steve asks, "You're going to Southern, aren't you?"

I've been having second thoughts about Southern and am now torn between going there and Creston. I choose my words carefully. "I'm planning to go to college in the fall."

"Well," Steve concludes, turning his palms upward. "There's no problem. Just let the draft board know that, they'll give you a 2-S, and you're set." With that Steve digs back into his food.

For me, the conversation hangs at a critical point. If I don't respond, the subject will change and I may not get another chance to talk about it before I register.

"No, I won't be set," I reply with an edge in my voice. "I'd just have to decide somewhere else along the line. Besides, I've heard that if you wait, it's harder to get a 1-0 classification. I guess I'd like to decide once and for all."

Steve speaks with a mouthful of food. "So decide. What's stopping you? Why hassle *us* about it?" In a subtle way, Steve creates a rift between me and the rest of the group. If there's to be a next word it will have to come from someone else. Matt saves the day.

"It may not be important to you, Steve, but it is to me. And, unless your memory's failing, you'll recall that we've talked about this subject more than once in the past. And we had some pretty good discussions. Now we're too busy burying our noses in beer cans to think about anything. I say something's wrong when we bite Jon's head off for just bringing the subject up."

Matt's words give Allen courage. "Yeah," Allen echoes. "I've been thinking about this, too. My birthday is only two weeks after Jon's. I've made up two lists—one with reasons to go 1-A and one with reasons for going 1-O. I'd like to see us decide this as a group. I don't want just to get a student deferment and then have to worry about what I'm going to do when I finish college."

"You'll be worrying about something," Steve says offhandedly. "It might as well be the draft."

Ignoring Steve's remark, Denny adds his thoughts. "I know what you mean," he says fervently. "Not knowing can drive you crazy. When we talk about this at youth group, I think I'll go 1-O. But then when Jack Griffin talks to me, I lean toward 1-A." Denny has a way of displaying his wishy-washy nature by being honest about it.

I stare at Denny. "When has Jack been talking to you?" Jack is a large, potbellied, red-haired man with two talents—one for drinking and the other for intimidating weaker spirits.

"Oh, off and on," Denny shrugs. "Sometimes I ride

around with him and we talk."

The thought of Jack influencing Denny angers me and I speak without thinking. "If I wanted to consider the merits of going into the army, I wouldn't spend my time talking to someone who spent all his time in the service loafing around German bars and whorehouses."

Denny flushes and looks at the ground. Steve looks up at me grinning broadly.

A sudden snore breaks the tension. During the course of the conversation, Chuck has fallen asleep.

Steve holds a finger to his lips to quiet us. He takes whipped cream from a plastic container in his lunch box and places it in Chuck's open palm. Then he pulls a blade of glass and begins to tickle Chuck's nose, imitating the movements of an insect.

Splat! We roar with laughter. Chuck adds to the comedy by licking the cream off his hand and face.

The foreman toots his horn to call us back to the fields. We gobble our remaining food, gather up our plastic bags, Tupperware containers, pop cans, and empty sacks and head back to our rigs.

Allen catches up with me. "You have any plans tonight?" he asks. "I thought we might get together."

"Saturday nights are reserved for Donna."

"Is that so?" Allen replies. He gives me a mysterious grin and jogs to his rig.

Back in the field I analyze the lunchtime conversation. I thought it was a pretty good conversation for a change. I kick myself for ending the talk with a stupid crack about Jack. But it needed to be said, I rationalize.

I decide not to give the matter any more thought for a while. Let the computer sort through the facts and come up with an answer. This afternoon we're going over a new field so I concentrate on being a perfect crew boss. The foreman would be ecstatic if he could see the way my squinting eyes dart back and forth, searching for broken tassels. Upon spotting one, I stop the machine and with set jaw and pointed finger send the offender back to the scene of the crime.

*   *   *

I plan my evening with Donna while taking a long and well-deserved shower.

I decide that tonight will be the night I bring our relationship out in the open, and I'll be on the offensive. Maybe Donna does like Steve, but, after all, I'm the one she's dating. All I have to do is assert myself a little and she'll forget he ever existed. I work a plan out in my mind. I'll take command from the start. I'll grasp her by the hand, lead her into the cedar-lined den, seat her on the sofa, stare into her eyes, and declare, "Donna, if we're going to have a relationship, I think it's time we set some things straight."

I cruise slowly along the country roads leading to the Timmons' house. The slowly setting sun and the relaxed chirping of crickets and tree toads inspire me.

Donna is radiant as she meets me at the door. I take her hand and, without resistance, lead her to the den. I open the swinging doors and fumble for the lights.

"Surprise! Surprise!"

People jump out from behind chairs, bookcases, and curtains, and begin to sing, "Happy birthday." Donna kisses me lightly on the cheek, then heads for the stereo.

Denny comes up behind me and whacks me on the back. "Hey, Jon ol' buddy. When you don't go out with us, we come to you." I can smell a trace of beer on his breath.

Allen walks up and shakes my hand. "Happy birthday, even if it is a few days early."

"Is the whole gang here?" I ask, looking around.

"Yep, everybody except Steve. He'd be here except he had a date he couldn't break."

"Since when can't Steve break a date?"

"Since he spent twenty bucks for tickets to a concert." Allen heads over to the refreshment table.

I sink back onto the sofa and listen to the music filtering through the chatter of the party. It's a song from the Beatles' album, *Abbey Road:*

> Once there was a way to get back homeward,
> Once there was a way to get back home.
> Sleep pretty darling do not cry,
> And I will sing a lullaby.
> Boy you're gonna carry that weight,
> Carry that weight a long time.
> Boy you're gonna carry that weight,
> Carry that weight a long time. . . .

CHAPTER 8

"Hey, just because you got in late last night doesn't mean you can spend all morning in the bathroom. The rest of us have to get ready for church too." My kid brother Dave pounds the door one last time and stomps away.

I lean close to the mirror and leisurely examine the straggly blond hairs that dot my chin and neck. I reluctantly pronounce judgment on these welcome intruders, apply dabs of lather, and perform the execution. One of the newest hairs manages to survive by its flimsiness. I poise the razor to perform delicate surgery.

"Ouch!" A fine line of red appears in place of the hair. I dab at the slow-oozing blood with a clot of toilet paper.

Martha knocks on the door. "Jon, we're ready for devotions. Hurry or the food will get cold." I dab one last time at the red smear on my chin.

"I see you've had your monthly shave," Dad teases as I slide into my seat at the table.

"How many times have I told you that when you find a hair, you are supposed to cut it off, not dig it out?" Martha adds with an irritating toss of her head. I yawn to let them know how much they're getting to me. Dad clears his throat, a signal that he's ready to begin.

Dad reads the account of the arrest of Jesus from Matthew 26: " . . . And, behold, one of them which were with Jesus stretched out his hand, and drew his sword, and struck a servant of the high priest's, and smote off his ear. Then said Jesus unto him, Put up again thy sword into his place: for all they that take the sword shall perish with the sword" (vv. 51-52).

Dad focuses his steely-gray eyes on me. "Choosing between the sword and the path that Jesus calls us to follow has never been a simple choice. It's easy to think that in this day and age the issues are much more complex and, therefore, the decisions harder. But the choice remains between good or evil. That was the choice Cain made when he slew Abel. From that day forth, man has possessed a violent nature and has too often been ready to resort to bloodshed."

Becky and Jim, the little ones, begin to squirm impatiently. Mom settles them with a stern look.

Dad goes on. "There are many things in life that on the surface may seem worth defending with violence. One that we hear most commonly in this country is freedom. We are told by some that the world is full of evil people whose goal is to overthrow our system and replace it with an oppressive one. But even in the days of the hated Roman Empire Jesus taught and lived the fact that oppression can be overthrown only by love and that true freedom can only be bought with the blood of the Lamb. Each of us must choose for himself whether he will take up the sword or whether he will follow the way and the will of the Son of God."

Our family spills from the car in the parking lot behind

the ungainly structure known as the Spireville Mennonite Church. The church building is a comedy of hybrid architecture. The main structure, built early in the century, resembles a huge barn with windows cut out as an afterthought. The educational wing, added only five years ago, is a modern, low-slung structure of glass, steel, and stained wood. This wing juts from the side of the old auditorium as if stuck there in a storm by a mischievous tornado.

I join Denny, Matt, and Allen who stand making small talk on the front lawn of the church. We keep an eye out for Steve's red Mustang. We wait until church is just about to start before giving up and going in. The worship leader starts to rise, sees us enter, and pauses until we are settled in the benches reserved for youth.

Deciding to have reserved seats for the youth was a minor milestone in the life of our congregation. Until last year, some unspoken code had dictated that women sit on the left side of the auditorium and men on the right. Locating a co-ed section in the middle of the right side of the auditorium disrupted this pattern of segregation and now males and females mingle in random, unartistic patterns.

The worship leader completes his opening and calls for the song leader. I know without checking the church bulletin that he will have prepared five songs—three before the devotional, two after. The song leader asks the congregation to turn to number 449. Matt and I begin our patented game—hymnal golf. I lead off. Using my right-hand thumbnail I make my first attempt and open the book at 427. An excellent first shot. Matt is not so lucky and ends up on 368. Using the rules of golf, Matt must keep going until he gets within my try. He succeeds on the next turn—hitting 456. On my second try I wind up on page 441. Now we both are within putting distance. This means that you can count the pages without looking. There is chance in this since some spreads contain two songs, some three, and a few four. Since I am outside Matt's shot, I go again. Luck isn't with me and I wind up a page short. Matt's putting is more accurate. He hits 449 on his third attempt—winning this round. I notice the name of the song is "Peace in Our Time, O Lord."

To my surprise, the devotional passage is the same that Dad used for our family worship. Since the devotional passage always accompanies the message, I open the bulletin on my lap to check the sermon title. "Blessed Are the Peacemakers" stares back at me. One of the fringe benefits of being a preacher, I think, is that you can address your offspring in front of an entire congregation and be blessed by God and others for your effort.

At precisely 9:55, after two more songs, Dad stands up, strides to the pulpit, opens his Bible, and begins to preach. Just as precisely, at 10:35, he will offer a closing prayer and return to the bench.

Dad opens with the peacemaker beatitude and then moves into the usual three points of his sermon. With extra fervor, I slide into my usual role as devil's advocate.

Dad begins by dealing with conflict in the Old Testament. He describes how God's people achieved their victories. The Philistines were defeated by a small boy with a slingshot. Joshua caused Jericho to fall by marching around it seven times for seven days bearing God's ark. When Gideon raised an army of 22,000 against the Midianites, God told him it was too large. Gideon was instructed to let all those that were afraid go home. All but 10,000 did. But God said that was still too many. So the

Lord led the army to water and told Gideon that only those that drank a certain way would fight. A mere 300 qualified and the rest were sent home. Then God used these 300 to route the Midianites, not by engaging in combat, but frightening them by blowing trumpets and breaking pitchers.

"In all these incidents, God left no doubt that the victory was his. I'm afraid, however, that God could not make such a claim for a nation armed with a doomsday arsenal of missiles, tanks, napalm, and nuclear warheads."

My mind gives its counterargument. You can't assume that just because weapons aren't the same today that war is fundamentally different. After all, the Israelites carried the most advanced weapons available in their day. If tanks had been invented, they certainly would have driven them into battle. They wouldn't have fought the enemy with slingshots.

Maybe all modern wars aren't right, but there must have been some in Old Testament times that weren't either. Besides, what about World War II where millions of Jews were being charred in furnaces? Was it the right Christian response to serve in some nice hospital in America, helping people overcome allergies and recover from gall bladder operations—while Hitler ran wild over in Europe?

Dad shifts to his second point. His booming reverberations from the loudspeakers nestled in the rafters unfairly overpower my thoughts. "Reading from Matthew 5, verse 38, Jesus says, 'Ye have heard that it hath been said, An eye for an eye, and a tooth for a tooth: but I say unto you, That ye resist not evil: but whosoever shall smite thee on thy right cheek, turn to him the other also.' Continuing in verse 44, Jesus says, 'Love your enemies, bless them that curse you, do good to them that hate you, and pray for them which despitefully use you, and persecute you; that ye may be the children of your Father which is in heaven." Passage after passage, Dad piles it on.

When it comes to proof-texting, Dad has me at a definite disadvantage. I don't know the references nearly as well. I flip through the pages of my Bible. Aha! What about Matthew 10, verse 34? "Think not that I am come to send peace on earth: I came not to send peace, but a sword. For I am come to set a man at variance against his father . . . ." I read on and my counterargument collapses. Jesus seems to mean that true love and obedience to him must be greater than our love and loyalty to other things, including our own families.

But what about all the consorting Jesus did with persons in the military? When soldiers responded to Jesus, he didn't require them to sign statements claiming to be conscientious objectors. He ate with captains and healed the sick daughter of a distraught officer. But this argument also starts to cave in as I think how Jesus associated with everyone from tax collectors to prostitutes, much to the disdain of the religious folks of his day. Jesus asserted that human beings were important and redeemable—whatever their lot in life.

Dad moves on to his third and final point—the example of our Anabaptist forefathers. He begins by stating the beliefs of the Anabaptists concerning war and armed service. Although most Christians of the time claimed to be against war, a "just-war" theory had evolved. This meant that if you could come up with a good enough reason for fighting in a particular war, it was all right to go into combat. Christian leaders of the time always found such a reason to justify their actions.

The Anabaptists took the unpopular stance that since wars were fought between nations for sovereignty, participating in them was a form of nation worship and, therefore, idolatry. They believed that the church, to be effective, must be separate from the state. The choice, they claimed, was between two kingdoms, that of this world and that of God. In choosing God, the Anabaptists, therefore, chose not to participate in fighting. Dad anticipates a counterargument and dismisses as misguided renegades the Anabaptists who by force took and defended the city of Munster.

Dad's booming voice drops to a choked whisper. A hush falls over the congregation as he opens a faded copy of *Martyrs Mirror*. The overhead spotlights reflect a halo of light off his sweating forehead. The brittle pages crinkle as he selects the passages. In a quiet but passionate voice Dad reads the accounts of men and women who witnessed for Christ, were tried, and put to death for their faith. The gruesome accounts that have appealed to me — mainly for their vivid details of drownings, burnings, and tortures — take on a new meaning as I see in them a reflection of the love and suffering of Christ.

I find myself almost envying these martyrs. Their situations seemed so clear and obvious. How could there possibly be ambiguities in such faith? For them, it was Christ or the world. Life or death. Or was it?

One story in particular sticks with me. In 1569, a man named Dirck Willems was fleeing from persecutors. He crossed an ice-covered stream safely but his first pursuer fell in. All the others stopped on the other side. Dirck was free to go on his way. But he turned and helped the man from the freezing water. In spite of this, he was arrested,

92

imprisoned, tortured, and burnt to death. I am moved by this incredible and unselfish expression of love. Dad closes the huge volume with a dramatic thud. The testimonies have stripped me of all counter-arguments—at least for the time being.

Dad concludes the sermon. "Our history of peace did not stop in the seventeenth century. Neither did our trials. In 1931 the Supreme Court of this land decided that conscientious objection was not an inalienable right. The effects of this decision were strongly felt during and after World War II by many of you here. You were called to put your faith into practice.

"And yes, even today, we are called to be peacemakers. Our response may be refusing to join a military machine that requires us to be ready to kill other human beings, or it may be in the way we treat our neighbors. Our every response must be weighed as if it was a response to Christ himself, the One who said in Matthew 25:40, 'Inasmuch as ye have done it unto one of the least of these my brethren, ye have done it unto me.' Would we be as willing to squeeze the trigger of a gun if Christ Himself were lined up in the sights? Would we be as willing to enlarge our fields by plowing into our neighbor's land if that neighbor were our Lord Jesus? Let us pray."

I glance at my watch. It is 10:38.

* * *

Sunday dinner is a family gathering at my grandparents'. Here we Mennonites will succumb to our one admitted vice—overeating. Warm welcomes resound throughout the cozy house at each new arrival. The soprano chatter of the women gravitates toward the

93

kitchen while the baritone laughter of the men moves into the only room I've ever been in that can properly be called a parlor. The men spread out comfortably in the overstuffed chairs that encircle the room. Martha, Dave, Jim, Becky, and I, along with our cousins, claim the throw pillows and squeeze into the remaining nooks and crannies.

Dad's sermon has stimulated memories of the hardships Mennonites in Illinois faced during World War II. Small towns such as Spireville, it seems, could muster vast amounts of patriotism. Being a pacifist and speaking German was like going to bat with two strikes against you.

My uncle tells an old story that, for me, takes on new intensity. "The gang of toughies from town—you know, Albert and his boys—they told me at school one day that until I say the 'Pledge of Allegiance' with the rest of the class, they're going to come out to the farm and paint a big yellow stripe on the shed for every day of school I don't pledge. Well, they did, too. For two weeks straight, they came out. After that everybody driving past could see ten big yellow lines on the side of our shed. My teacher told me not to worry since she doubted if any of 'em could count to twenty." Several of the men chuckle.

"Well, one night all us boys got together with brushes and ladders and painted that whole shed yellow." The room explodes in laughter.

"You should've seen their faces the next day when they came out with their paint and all."

I look closely at my uncle's face and see the pain etched between the lines of laughter.

"Yep," Gramps sighs, "but things weren't always so funny. Remember the time that gang caught the young Birky boy?" The men nod somberly. Gramps gazes across

94

the room, out the window.

"Well, what happened?" Dave asks, busting with curiosity.

Gramps says he doesn't want to go into it, but persistent urging finally breaks his resistance. He tells the story briefly and without flourishes. I remember the story only vaguely, so I listen intently.

"Well, this Birky feller was out weedin' fence rows one day when these ruffians come along in an old jalopy. They took after him, caught him, and knocked him to the ground. While three of 'em held him face down, another took a needle and sewed a little American flag right on the part of him that you and me uses for sittin'." The young ones break out in giggles.

"It wasn't funny at all," Gramps continues sternly. "They used an old rusty needle to do it. He got a bad infection and nearly lost a leg. Never could walk as good after that." The room falls silent a moment in tribute.

The reminiscing continues. The cruel irony was that conscientious objectors were often stationed on or near military bases. Few of their experiences would have made *Martyrs Mirror*, but they still tried the faith of young boys just off the farm and away from home for the first time. The tribulations ranged from being spit on and having to scrub latrines with a toothbrush to being the victims of such practical jokes as having the legs of their cots sawed through or finding bed lice in their food. A strong faith, quiet dignity, and a sense of humor were the only weapons the conscientious objectors had for surviving such experiences with their spirits intact.

At the dinner table, two of my uncles pretend to be looking for something in their food. Grandma asks them what on earth are they doing. When one replies that

95

they're looking for bed lice, the men break into gales of knee-slapping laughter.

* * *

I have been given the evening off from church—a rare privilege—to go see Donna. I knock on her door and peer cautiously inside when she opens it.

"Don't worry," she laughs. "I don't have any more surprises in store for you." Her family, however, is home and in the middle of an argument over which TV program to watch. Donna suggests that we go for a long walk together.

We stroll hand in hand down a grassy path separating a soybean field from corn. At the edge of a pasture we find a place to relax under a cluster of trees. I lean back against the broad trunk of an oak. Donna sits next to me, resting her head on my shoulder. We chat idly for a while about anything and everything. Slowly I muster the courage to unload the issue that has been burdening me all day. During a long pause, I make the leap.

"Donna, if two people are really close, they should be able to share things—deep things—with each other, shouldn't they?"

"Sure, I guess." Donna straightens up. "What's on your mind?"

"It's the whole draft thing. Since I turn 18 this week, I have to register." Donna nods blankly. I search for the words that will help her understand the turmoil that has been building up inside me.

"Well, once you register for the draft, you have to decide things—like whether or not you're going to join the Army."

"My Dad says that the Navy is better," Donna replies.

I decide to take a more direct tack.

"Donna, you know I'm a Mennonite, don't you?"

"Sure."

"Well, Mennonites have certain beliefs about things. Like war, for instance. Most Mennonites don't believe in fighting and killing."

"I guess I wouldn't want to go to war and get all shot up, either."

"No, it's not that we want to keep from getting shot up, it's. . . ."

"Oh, Jon," Donna pleads. "Do we have to talk about things like that tonight? I mean, it's so depressing. Let's just be happy."

* * *

On Tuesday, thunderstorms sweep across the flat plains of Illinois. Since we can't work in the fields, I take the opportunity to register at the draft board. While waiting in line, I thumb through a brochure on the history of the draft. The brochure opens, ironically, with a passage from the Bible, Numbers 1:1-3, which it claims was the first draft:

> And the Lord spake unto Moses in the wilderness of Sinai, in the tabernacle of the congregation, on the first day of the second month, in the second year after they were come out of the land of Egypt, saying Take ye the sum of all the congregation of the children of Israel, after their families, by the house of their fathers, with the number of their names, every male by their polls; from twenty years old and upward, all that are able to go forth to war in Israel: thou and Aaron shall number them by their armies.

Registration proves to be uneventful. No big decisions here. I simply fill in my name, address, occupation, birth date, and other trivia. A tired-looking clerk hands me Selective Service Form No. 100, my classification questionnaire, and tells me to return it within a week.

* * *

That night I sit thoughtfully at my desk and go over the questionnaire. Again, for the most part, the form is undramatic. Numbers one through seven deal with basic and uncontroversial data. Number eight, however, reads, "I claim to be a conscientious objector by reason of my religious training and belief and therefore request the board to furnish me a special form for conscientious objector status (SSS Form No. 150)." There it is. A simple statement, a box to check, and a blank to sign. If I don't check the box and sign my name, I can send the form back in and my registration process is complete. I'll be classified 1-A just like 99 percent of all the other guys who register. But, if I do sign. . . .

* * *

I twist and turn in bed, sweating in spite of an open window and rotating fan. My mind is a jury weighing the presentations of two slick-tongued lawyers who have engaged in debate worthy of Lincoln and Douglas. The interrogations and cross-examination have gone on for days. The final presentations have been made and the jury isolates itself to wrestle with the verdict.

The most persistent juror is a lanky, blondish fellow. His face gleams with sweat as he states, "No one short of

God can understand anything completely. That is why we were given more than intellect. That is why we have emotions and a conscience. Sometimes you have to move beyond rational thought and do the thing that you feel in your heart is right."

The jury returns to the courtroom. The foreman stands, unfolds a piece of paper, and starts to read the verdict. "We, the jury, find . . . ."

I leap out of bed, spread the classification questionnaire out under my desk light, and make my decision. I seal the form in its envelope, return to bed, and lapse into sleep.

CHAPTER 9

"This parade," the mayor's voice squawks through mushroom shaped speakers, "is dedicated to the red, white, and blue and to those in Spireville who served under our waving banner. For those heroes red meant courage, white meant purity, and blue—honor."

Bang! The mayor lays the still-smoking pistol on the podium and the Fourth of July parade begins.

Sweating in their heavy wool outfits, the high school band leads off. Matt and I standing with our families, wave and grin at acquaintances as they march along Main Street. The band's rendition of the "Star-Spangled Banner" sounds thin and strained in the open-air setting.

Children on decorated tricycles follow the band. They are the most popular feature of the parade and loud applause marks their progress. Antique cars sporting small flags are next. After the cars, come the floats representing the civic organizations and churches of Spireville—minus, of course, the Mennonite church.

One float bears a large copy of the Bill of Rights at one end and the Ten Commandments at the other. Two children stand in the middle—one dressed as Moses and the other as Uncle Sam. As the float passes, Moses grabs

Uncle Sam's hat and puts it on his own head. The crowd laughs and applauds this antic.

The middle of the parade is reserved for the fire engines and police cars. They pass in a clamor of sirens, horns, and flashing lights that resemble an invasion from outer space.

Coach Dudding, this year's parade marshall, sits perched atop the final fire engine. He smiles, waves to the crowd, and tosses wrapped candy onto the sidewalk for the kids to scamper after. As he approaches us, he reaches into his bag for another handful of goodies. His arm stops in midair and his grin quickly disappears as he spots Matt and me. He looks away while his hand continues its motion. Candy flies through the air, landing in the gutter and scattering into the street. Matt, Dave, and I have to restrain our younger brothers and sisters from going after it.

The Cassel County Horse Club provides the grand finale to the parade. The club appeared for the first time last year and, mistakenly, had been placed in front of the tots on trikes. The crowd had gone into hysterics as several youngsters had aimed their vehicles deliberately through the piles of freshly dropped dung.

After the parade, Matt and I jump into the Blue Beast and head for the next attraction of the day, the annual Fourth of July picnic in Sutter's pasture. Originally planned as a Mennonite alternative to the town's celebration, the picnic has become yet another Spireville ritual over the Fourth. The quality of Mennonite cooking and the ferocity of the slow-pitch softball tournament attracts Spireville residents of all backgrounds. Originally, the picnic had begun with an hour-long worship service focusing on the nonresistant way of life. In recent years, however, this has been reduced to a brief, nonoffensive devotional just before eating.

"I take it you're going to watch the fireworks with Donna tonight," Matt says.

"Yeah, I guess so." Having a date to watch the fireworks is virtually a requirement of Spireville social life.

"For a guy that's going steady, you don't sound overly excited about it." I glance down at the white strip around my finger where my ring has been until recently.

"What do you want me to do, break out into a hot sweat?"

"Sorry I said anything. By the way, where is Donna's ring?"

"At home on my dresser."

"She'll kill you if she sees you're not wearing it."

"Her family went to visit relatives for the afternoon. I'll have it on by tonight. By the way, who are you taking to the fireworks?"

"I finally asked Connie."

"Really? Not bad."

Matt turns into Sutter's dirt lane and we rumble toward the gathering picnickers, trailed by a cloud of dust. The women fan away the dust that drifts toward the food, complaining good-naturedly as we pass to park the car.

By noon, several hundred people have arrived and the picnic starts. Dad reads a short passage from the Bible and recites St. Francis of Assissi's "Prayer for Peace."

Lord, make me an instrument of Thy peace.
Where there is hate, may I bring love;
Where offense, may I bring pardon;
May I bring union in place of discord;
Truth, replacing error;
Faith, where once there was doubt;
Hope, for despair;

102

Light, where was darkness;
Joy to replace sadness.
Make me not to so crave to be loved as to
     love.
Help me to learn that in giving I may receive;
In forgetting self, I may find life eternal.

As soon as the word "Amen" is spoken, the youngsters swarm around the tables like ants. For all their activity, they do little to deplete the ample resources that have been spread out. Next, we teenagers make our raid. The adults hang back, chatting in small groups, secure in the knowledge that the heavily laden tables bear more food than twice their number of offspring could consume.

Dessert is ice-cream bars packed in dry ice. Youngsters fill empty cans with nearby pond water, pirate small chunks of the ice, immerse them in the water, and watch in awe as smokelike fumes billow forth.

When all the food has been eaten or packed away, two softball fields are marked off with trails of lime. Several men place folding chairs along the sidelines for those who by inclination or better judgment choose not to participate in the tournament.

Matt, Steve, Allen, and myself are given the honor of picking the four teams that will compete. We roll balls from the pitcher's mound toward home plate. The one who comes the closest gains the right to choose first. My ball stops a foot short of home plate, almost a sure bet to win. Steve throws too hard, but his ball collides with mine, sending it the farthest from the plate. Steve's ball stops dead in its tracks beside the plate. The crowd cheers and I manage a grin. When I get my first choice, I pick Denny, the best catcher around.

Steve's team plays Matt's and I compete with Allen's in

the first-round, five-inning games. Both games are hard fought. When the dust clears, Steve's team and mine are the victors. After a short break for lemonade, the seven-inning championship game gets under way.

The first five innings belong to my team. We take a commanding 17 to 6 lead. In five at bats, I contribute a home run and two singles to the cause. Even more satisfying is the leaping catch I make of Steve's hard-hit line drive in the fourth inning.

In the sixth, however, my concentration starts to slip. I don't know whether to blame the heat, our comfortable lead, Steve's icy stares, or my own wandering thoughts. At bat, I kill a rally by tapping a ball back to the pitcher and ending the inning.

In the field, at shortstop, my glove turns into a wet noodle. Steve, leading off the inning, seems to sense my distraction. Being a good place hitter he lines a shot to my right. I react slowly and lunge at the ball. It nicks my glove, caroming off into the left field. His team bats around, narrowing the gap. At bat again later in the same inning, Steve sends another line drive in my direction. I leap for the ball, missing the catch but knocking it down. Too late to force the runners advancing to second and third, I fire quickly to first. My throw goes wild, scattering spectators and scoring two more runs.

The momentum of the game has shifted. In the top of the seventh, my side is retired in order, bringing Steve's team up to bat. We still retain a slim, three-run lead. The first batter walks, followed by a guy who clobbers a home run. The third hitter singles, and the fourth and fifth batters walk to load the bases. We take time out to change pitchers and plan strategy. The next player smashes a grounder in my direction. I field the ball cleanly and

104

throw home for the force out. One away.

Now Steve is at bat. I pound my glove hoping Steve will again test my reflexes which are back to needle sharp. Steve swings at the first pitch and pops a deep foul back of third base. Since the third baseman is playing in, I have the best chance for it. I'm off in a flash, streaking for the rapidly descending sphere. Running at top speed, I stretch for the ball. I catch it in the outer web of my glove's pocket. But suddenly the thick trunk of a tree looms in front of me.

Smack! Fourth of July fireworks shoot off in my head and I taste blood in my mouth. I shake my head to clear my senses and see to my relief that the ball is still in my glove. The crowd is hollering at the top of their lungs and in my shaken state it takes me too long to realize why. With only two outs, the runners on second and third have tagged up and are heading for home. The second runner has rounded third by the time I rear back to throw. Denny does his best to block the plate until the ball arrives. But my throw is too high and the winning run slides safely under his swooping tag.

With the game over, the adults settle under the shade to swap stories, while the youngsters head off to explore the pond and the far corners of Sutter's pasture. Matt, Steve, Chuck, Denny, Allen, and I pile into the Blue Beast and head for town.

The Fourth of July carnival in the town park is the pride and joy of Spireville. It has always been the biggest celebration in Cassel County. The large number of side attractions and the variety of the carnival rides attracts people from all corners of the county and beyond.

The Spireville park consists of a quarter-mile stretch of blacktop road with a wooded section on one side and three adjoining ball parks on the other. Concession stands and sideshows dot the wooded section. An old bandstand surrounded by bleachers is transformed into a stage for country-Western bands, a talent show, and the traditional hog-calling contest. Two of the ball diamonds are covered with music-blaring, whirling, twirling, stomach churning rides.

At dusk the rides and concession stands will be shut down and the third ballfield lit by the "biggest and most patriotic display of fireworks in central Illinois" —or so the posters say.

We park the Blue Beast and stroll up and down the park road which has been barricaded to become a broadway for foot traffic only. A huge banner stretches across the road proclaiming: "Cassel County Charity Carnival." For the last several years, the proceeds of the Fourth of July carnival have gone to various county charities instead of local merchants. One result of this change has been that Mennonites who once avoided the carnival now help to organize it.

I spend a quarter to try and douse an already soaked girl in the dunk tank. On my second throw, I hit the target, dropping her into the cold water.

"If you had thrown home like that this afternoon, we might have won the game," Denny kids.

Munching hot dogs, we watch the end of the talent show. The hog-calling contest begins and we are conned into participating. "Don't worry," the master of ceremonies assures us, "there'll be a sheet in front of you so no one can tell who it is."

The sheet turns out to be a three-foot square piece of cloth with the face of a pig drawn on it. Since people surround the platform, the few that cannot see the

106

contestant's face can be quickly informed of his identity.

"Sue-e-e-e-e!" we all holler in turn, varying only in volume, tone, emphasis, and credibility. Denny gives in to the inevitable temptation. "Here piggy, piggy, piggy," he coos.

The winner is determined by a gadget that records applause level. Matt and I, the only ones who have any actual experience calling hogs, come in second and third to a grade school music teacher who "suees" up and down the scale in perfect pitch.

We leave the festivities and head to the local gas station, where Allen works, for a quiet game of cards. Since nobody seems in the mood for cards, we abandon the effort after a few futile hands. We sit back on tractor tires and cardboard boxes drinking bottles of pop and discussing our evening plans.

"Hey, Denny," Chuck asks, "did you ever get Karen what's-her-name to go to the fireworks with you?"

"Yeah," Denny says. "I'm going to pick her up at nine when the concessions close down."

"Which one's she working at?"

"The dunk tank." Denny hesitates.

"All right! She's going to need someone to warm her up." We razz Denny and he flushes with embarrassment and pride.

The rest of us give our reports. I nod my head to confirm I'll be with Donna. Allen hasn't decided between two girls. Denny makes the helpful suggestion that since both options are lackluster, he should take them both. Chuck is going with some girl from another town that none of us know. Matt reports he'll be with Connie. All eyes turn to Steve.

Steve coyly spins a pop bottle on the cement floor.

"C'mon, Steve, who'd you pick from your black book for tonight?" Denny asks.

Steve shrugs. "Let's have it, Steve," Chuck says, "the rest of us confessed."

Steve stops playing with the bottle and straightens up. "There's nothing to confess."

"What do you mean by that?"

Steve is clearly enjoying this game of 20 questions. "It's as simple as it sounds," he remarks. "I don't have a date."

"You're going to get one, aren't you?"

"Oh, I figure I'll hang around the park and see what happens."

"That's taking a chance. Any girl worth going with is taken by this time."

Steve shrugs and smiles. "Could be, but I feel lucky today."

* * *

Matt drops me off at home and I prepare for my evening date with Donna. After showering and dressing, I go to the dresser for the final touch. I open my top drawer and remove a fine, sterling silver chain. I pass the chain from palm to palm, feeling the coolness of the metal links. The piece of jewelry cost me $17.00—more than I've ever spent for a luxury item in my entire life.

I take Donna's ring from the dresser top and slip it onto the chain. Then, after several fumbled attempts, I fasten the chain around my neck. I debate whether to wear the ring over my shirt or under it. I decide to wear it under my shirt—at least until I am out of sight of my family.

For this occasion, I have been given Dad's new black Volkswagon to drive. The ride to the Timmons residence is a smooth, quiet one—without the bone-jarring rattles from the rutted roads that I am used to in the Plymouth.

I feel the lump under my shirt to make sure Donna's ring is in place. I still can't believe that Donna and I are really going steady. When I asked her, I figured she would at least want to think it over for a day or so. Instead, she had agreed right away—well, at least the same evening.

Now, for the first time since Donna and I have been dating, I am almost beginning to believe that our relationship is for real—that she wants to be with me because I'm me, not just to get at someone else. The thought puts me in high spirits. Yes sir, this may just be the greatest evening of my life! I lay on the horn as I swing into her drive.

Donna bursts through the front door like the evening's first firework. She is decked out, appropriately, in a navy blue pantsuit with bold red and white stripes. I notice immediately that she is wearing my ring. She has tucked white fur around the band to hold the ring in place on her smaller finger.

She slides in next to me and we are off for the carnival.

Spireville Park is by now overflowing with festive people. The park road is crammed with strolling couples, racing kids, and conversing adults. Donna and I mingle in the stream of traffic, greeting and chatting with acquaintances, then excusing ourselves and going on our way. Once we run into Steve, ambling along by himself.

We stand in line to ride the most popular attraction at this year's carnival—the Big Tilt. The ride consists of a long, fluorescently lit beam that revolves, supporting a ring of carriages on each end that also rotate. The rotating of the carriages, combined with the revolving and tilting of the main beam, provides countless variations of hair-raising thrills. Donna and I climb into a cage and lock ourselves in.

Lights start to flash, music begins to play, and the carriages accelerate. "Just think if this thing would come loose while we're going," I tease.

"Oh Jon," she squeals in mock terror, "don't say things like that."

"Look at the bright side," I persist. "If our carriage does come loose, we'd have a good view of the fireworks." Donna clamps a hand firmly over my mouth. The ride picks up speed and the outside world becomes a blur of whirling lights and silhouettes. The centrifugal force squeezes us together at one side of the cage. My arms encircle and protect her. With one hand I steady her head against my shoulder. In spite of the whipping frenzy of the ride, I can feel a warm tremor run through her. She presses against me.

It's true, I think to myself. When you fall in love, you do hear music playing and see lights flashing.

The July evening grows dark and unseasonably cool. The rides comes to a halt; the concessions begin to close. Droves of people return to their cars and gather up lawn chairs and sweaters for viewing the fireworks. I join the stream and grab the old quilt in the back of the VW. I tuck it under my arm and begin to jog back to where I left Donna.

"Hey, Bob!" a voice calls. I continue on my way.

"Bob, Bob Dudding! Wait up!" A familiar ring in the voice stops me in my tracks. I turn in the direction of the voice. A shiny-faced girl in a loud green and orange outfit struggles toward me waving her arms. When she finally arrives, she's all out of breath. She grabs my arm for support. I try to back off and get a look at her. The girl takes a deep breath and looks up at me. Suddenly it hits me. Indiana Beach. The girl at the dance. What was her name? Marsha something. Oh yeah, Marsha Henderson. But what is she doing here?

"Surprised to see me?" she asks excitedly.

"Uh, y-y-yes I am," I stammer.

"I'll bet you're wondering how I found you," she says dramatically.

"How did you?" Suddenly I am angered at this strange and untimely turn of events. Before she can answer, Steve saunters up.

"Oh, I see you two lovebirds found each other." Marsha gives a toothy grin and hugs my arm more tightly.

Steve continues matter-of-factly. "Yeah, Bob, since you were always talking about Marsha—when I found out from Matt what her last name was and that she lived in Peoria, I thought to myself, 'Why not do a favor for an ol' pal?' So I went through the telephone directory and called every Henderson until, zappo, I hit the jackpot. "Well," he begins to move away, "you two have a wonderful time now." He grins broadly over his shoulder.

Steve has made a calculated gamble that I won't cause a scene. My wish not to get caught in the lie of the borrowed name strengthens his hand.

"By the way, Bob," Steve calls, "have you seen Donna around anywhere?" I glare at him mutely. "Well, never mind." He shrugs, then adds, "I'll find her somewhere." Steve turns and saunters off.

Marsha tugs at my arm to get my attention. "Isn't this great?" she gurgles. "And we were afraid we wouldn't ever see each other again."

For lack of anything better to do under the circumstances, I invite her to watch the fireworks that are about to start. I lead her behind the crowd that has gathered around the ball diamond to a clump of pine trees.

"Guess what?" Marsha exclaims when we are seated. "I still have that same hanky with me. Want to see it?" Without waiting for a reply or even reminding me what in the world she's talking about, she digs into her side pocket. A piece of folded paper falls to the ground.

"Oh, I almost forgot," Marsha gasps. "Steve handed me this note when he met me at the parking lot. He said I was to give it to you and that I wasn't to look at it under any circumstances. It must really be important."

I take the note from her and open it up. The message on the card reads: "All's fair!"

CHAPTER 10

"Did you hear Bob Dudding broke his leg yesterday?" Dad remarks at breakfast. I almost choke on a mouthful of cornflakes.

"How did that happen?"

"He was hauling some water for his cattle when he hit a washout."

"The way it sounds he's lucky even to be alive," Mom adds. "The tractor could have landed right on top of him."

"Who's going to take care of the farm now?" I ask.

"I don't know," Dad replies. "I thought I'd stop by the hospital on my rounds this morning and talk to him." We finish breakfast and head our various ways.

I drive past the Timmons house without stopping. After the incident on the Fourth, Donna and I—mostly Donna—decided to cool our relationship for a while. To make things easier, we agreed that she should switch crews. She traded places with Sharon Litwiller—a fact I resented at first. Sharon's buoyant personality and freckle-faced good humor, however, have been a big help to my crew in making it through the long, summer workdays.

The detasseling season has peaked and is on the

decline. Several crews have been laid off and those of us who remain have the dubious privilege of braving swarms of gnats and a scorching, mid-July sun for the remaining tassels which are on the verge of pollinating. The foreman's white cowboy hat can frequently be seen bobbing along the rows of corn as he searches for missed tassels.

The crews have been split up into scattered fields and it is rare now that our entire gang can get together at lunchtime. Today only Matt, Denny, Allen, and I eat together.

"Hey," Denny says, opening the conversation. "Did you know that Steve was over at Donna's again last night?" Even though the revelation doesn't surprise me, I feel a twinge of jealousy.

"If I were you," Allen adds, "I'd get back with her quick before Steve takes over completely."

"Knowing the dirty trick he pulled," Denny exclaims waving a half-eaten apple in the air, "I can't understand why she'll have anything to do with the rotten fink! You did tell her the whole story, didn't you?"

"We started to talk about it a couple of times," I say ruefully. "But the whole thing got pretty complicated, what with Indiana Beach, Marsha, and all." Breaking up really hurt for the first couple of weeks. Now, however, I am resigned to the situation and have accepted the fact that our separation is probably more than temporary. Surprisingly, I have experienced a sense of release. With my mind free from worrying about all the complexities of a romantic relationship, I have been able to turn my attention to some neglected issues.

Matt speaks up, interrupting my thoughts. "Look Jon, what happens between you and Donna is your business.

But what's happening to our group is all of our business. Since this Donna incident came along, the gang has started to split up. It's time we get things out in the open, before it's too late."

I clear my throat. "I couldn't agree with you more."

Matt continues. "Look, Chuck and I were talking, see, and we thought that maybe we should all get together tonight and try to work things out. What do you say?"

"Sounds good to me," I reply.

Matt looks at Denny and Allen. They both nod agreement. "It would be great to all get together again, just like old times," Allen adds.

"Okay, then it's settled," Matt says. "I'll pick you guys up about seven."

For a while, we eat in silence. One of the issues I have neglected is the draft question. The form for obtaining conscientious objector status that I requested arrived and I have begun to think about the matter again. I'd hoped that making the decision to ask for 1-0 status would put me at ease. This hasn't been the case, however. While I have worked through most of my ideas, I am still bothered by a sense that there are vast differences between what I say I believe and how I live. Not knowing where the rest of the gang is on this contributes to my uneasiness about the matter.

While driving the rig this morning, I decided to raise the whole question with the group one last time. Instead of just starting in cold, though, I worked up a plan to introduce the subject in a roundabout fashion. It's now or never, I think to myself.

"Y'know," I begin, "it's funny how when you're young you say a lot of crazy things you really don't mean."

"Like what?" Denny swallows the bait.

"Well, remember when we were in grade school and we all said that when we grew up we were going to a cabin in the mountains and spend the rest of our lives eating mashed potatoes? We said we'd take turn guarding the place so no girls could come near us."

"That's right." Denny laughs. "I'd still do it provided we let the girls get as close as they want!" I wait for things to quiet down again.

"And then there was the time when we studied South America our sophomore year. We were going to buy a van and drive down to Columbia to start a banana plantation."

Allen recalls when we all wanted to spend the summer bumming around the country on motorcycles. I steel myself for the clincher.

"And then there was the time," I state without particular expression, "that we decided we'd face this draft thing together." An uneasy silence falls over the group. I press the point.

"Maybe we were naive to think we would all decide the same, but we don't even talk about things like that any more. I've already had to register and return my classification questionnaire." I look at Allen. "You must have had to send yours in by now, too. What did you do?"

Allen squirms uncomfortably. "Well, like you say, we never really talked about it. I decided to just get my student deferment and worry about the other stuff later—if I have to." He looks away.

"That's what I mean," I continue. "We'll all end up putting this thing off and by the time we have to decide, we'll be split up. We may not even go to the same college for all we know."

"What do you mean by that?" Denny asks. "We're all going to Southern, aren't we?"

116

"I don't know," I reply. "I've been accepted at Creston and they gave me a pretty good scholarship." The conversation shifts to upcoming college plans. I let it drift for a minute, then interrupt.

"Look, we'll never get anywhere if we keep going off on tangents."

"What about you, Jon?" Matt asks. "You said you sent in your form but you didn't say what you finally decided."

I take a deep breath. "So far I've decided to go 1-0." I survey their faces to see how they react.

Matt speaks thoughtfully. "I've mulled this whole thing over some and I guess I'm with you, Jon. I know we should've talked about this more as a group, but I had to work something out for myself first—whether or not I wanted to be a Christian. What you said awhile back about not putting off decisions really hit me. I realized I was at a place in my life where I had to start deciding who I was and what I believed.

"So, to start with, I decided I really want to follow Christ. I'll admit I don't know what that all means, but I'm ready to learn and to change.

"The funny thing is, after I made that decision, the decision whether or not to go 1-0 was easy. Being ready to do what Christ would do made the answer obvious. Take, for instance, the passage in John where Jesus is on trial and he tells Pilate that his kingdom is not of this world and that if it were his followers would fight for him. If we say Jesus is the most important thing in our lives and if we shouldn't fight to protect Jesus, I don't know what else there is to fight for! All the time we were arguing about whether or not to be conscientious objectors, we should have been deciding whether or not to follow Christ." I look at Matt with new appreciation.

117

Denny seems to have been moved by Matt's speech. "Yeah, me too," he blurts. "I'm going to go 1-0 even if Steve and Chuck aren't."

I look at Denny in surprise. "How do you know they're not?"

Denny's embarrassment betrays the fact that he's let a cat out of the bag. "Look, don't say anything about this, okay? Soon after we got back from Indiana Beach, the three of us were riding around with Jack Griffin. He was kidding us about washing out bedpans instead of fighting like men. Both Steve and Chuck said that they weren't going to clean out nobody's bedpan and that if they got drafted they'd join the marines."

The lunch break ends too quickly. The revelation about Chuck and Steve combined with my own incomplete thoughts on the draft matter create an uneasy turmoil within me. I feel a sudden, urgent need to talk about the situation with someone.

I swallow a huge chunk of pride and yell down to Sharon Litwiller working in the far basket. "Hey, Sharon, can you talk?"

"Yeah, my parents said I started when I was eleven months old."

"Very funny. I mean can you talk now. I've got something on my mind."

"I'll do my best—as long as you don't mind me missing a few tassels now and then."

I have an inspiration. "Fred," I call. "You're always begging to drive this rig. How'd you like to trade places?" I don't have to ask twice.

"There," I say, as I jump into the basket alongside Sharon. "Now we can talk and work at the same time."

"What more could a girl ask for?" she replies.

118

I ignore her quip and begin pouring out my soul. I bring her up to date with all that has happened so far concerning the draft—my thoughts, feelings, and conversations with the other guys. Sharon listens attentively, commenting now and then to keep me from rambling. Finally I get to the current problem—Selective Service System Form No. 150, the required questionnaire for obtaining conscientious objector status that now lies incomplete upon my dresser.

"The first three questions aren't hard," I continue. "The first one asks you to describe your beliefs and how they are based on religious training. The second question asks how you came about your beliefs and who influenced you. The third one asks if you would serve in the army as a noncombatant. I'm not saying I have all the answers to these, but with a little help from Dad I can get by. It's question number four that has me stumped."

"What is it?"

"I've stared at it so often I've got it memorized. It reads: 'Have you ever given expression, publicly or privately, written or oral, to the views herein expressed as the basis for your claim? Give examples.' "

"So what's your problem?"

"It's just that I've never done that—never spoken up for my beliefs. Not when it really counts, anyway. How could I have? I haven't even been sure of my beliefs for very long. I'm afraid that when I try to answer the question, it's going to look like I'm going 1-0 just to stay out of the army."

"Well, are you?" Sharon levels her penetrating blue eyes at me.

"No, I'm not! Well . . . I guess that's really the problem. I'm not sure. I think I believe in peace, nonresistance, and all that. But, some of the things I've done make me feel like a first-rate hypocrite."

"Oh? What things?"

"Well, for instance, the way I carried on at Indiana Beach earlier this summer and some of the pranks I helped pull on Coach Dudding. I mean, we did some dirty stuff. Now, with Dudding laid up in the hospital, thinking of the pranks we pulled on him really gets to me."

"Then there's your chance."

"What do you mean by that?"

"You want a chance to express your peace position, don't you? With Coach Dudding, you'd have a captive audience."

"You mean go see Coach Dudding and apologize?"

"That would be too easy. I mean go to Coach Dudding and be a peacemaker."

"What's the difference?"

"Well, when Jesus saw somebody in need, did he just tell them how sorry he was?"

"I get what you're saying, but I'm the last person the coach'll want to see. He'll probably throw his Gideon's Bible at me. Then again. . . ."

"Hey! How do you turn this thing around?" Fred screams. We have come to the end of a row and are headed toward a soybean field. I scramble up into the seat, cut speed, hit the clutch, and swing the wheel. The right side of the machine cuts an arc through the end rows of beans. I demote Fred back to detasseller.

"Y'know, you're all right," I call down to Sharon as I head the rig back up the field.

"I'll bet you say that to all the girls," she replies.

"How'd you like to go out this weekend?" I ask on a

120

sudden impulse.

"That depends. With who?"

"With me."

"With someone as confused as you? Forget it." She pauses long enough for my ego to deflate, then adds, "However, if you can straighten yourself out by next weekend, I'll consider it."

Another day in the fields ends. I park my rig and trudge with my crew toward the car.

"Springer, step over here." Reluctantly I alter my course toward the foreman leaning against his truck. He fans himself with a bunch of tassels he holds in his hand. As I approach, he thrusts them in my direction.

"Y'know what these things are?"

Not this game again, I think to myself. "They look like tassels to me," I reply.

"I'm surprised you recognize them. I just found 'em in the field you supposedly finished." As big as the tassels are, I doubt whether my crew missed them. He continues, "Five tassels may not seem like much but when you think of millions of grains of pollen floating around the air, it adds up fast." With this reprimand, he drops the tassels and moves to the next subject.

"And another thing. I noticed you let one of your crew members drive the rig."

"Yes, sir."

"Don't you know that's against regulations?"

"I don't see what harm it did. In fact, it helped break the monotony."

"Monotony!" The foreman recoils from the word like it bit him. "Well, excuse the Frontier Seed Corn Company for boring you. In case you've forgotten, we pay you a pretty penny for your trouble. Maybe we should find

121

someone who appreciates that fact a little more." The foreman starts to turn away.

"Maybe you should, sir."

The foreman wheels to face me. "What did you say?"

"I said that if you're not happy with the work I'm doing, maybe you should get someone to replace me. You said once that you have a lot of people who want the job."

The foreman seems taken back by this turn of events. "Well, yeah, that's true. But this late in the season. . . ."

"I'll work until you find somebody," I reply evenly.

"Okay, okay. If that's how you feel about it, don't even bother coming tomorrow. I'll get somebody tonight." The foreman jumps in his truck, slams the door, and roars away.

For some strange reason the confrontation has lifted my spirits—no games, no beating around the bush. Just coming out and being honest about the situation.

Bolstered with my newfound courage, I drop off my ex-crew members and head for what may be my second confrontation.

I almost chicken out as I pull up in front of the hospital. But, I think of the stories in *Martyrs Mirror*. If people like Dirck Willems could risk their lives to follow Christ, I can probably risk a little uneasiness.

"Hello, Linda," I greet the receptionist. She peers up at me over her bifocals.

"Oh hello, Jon, are you back working here again?"

"No, nothing like that. I just heard that Coach Dudding was in the hospital and I thought I might stop in and see him."

"You should know that visiting hours don't start until six. You're ten minutes early."

"Well, then maybe I'll just wander around for

122

old-time's sake. What's his room number just in case I happen by?"

"Uh, 124. But if anybody asks, I didn't see you come in." She smiles and waves me on.

I find room 124 and knock on the door. "Who is it?" a gruff voice calls out.

"Jon." A long pause. "Jon Springer. Can I come in to see you for a minute, sir?"

"I'm resting."

"I won't take long." Dudding doesn't reply and I take that to be as close to an affirmative answer as I can expect. I push the door open. Dudding is sitting up with his huge arms folded in front of him and his broad shoulders set rigidly.

"What in the world do you *want?*" he asks in a stern voice.

"I heard about your accident," I begin. "I'm sorry about that and . . . and all the other things too."

"What other things?" I can tell by the tone of his voice that he knows what other things, but wants to hear me say it.

"Well, the way I acted in your class, and the pranks I helped pull this summer."

"An apology won't get me my tractor back."

"I know words aren't much help, but there is something I can do."

"What's that?" he asks looking straight at me.

"Well, with you on crutches for a while, I thought maybe I could help out at the farm. Until you get better, that is."

The coach's voice softens a little. "Well that's good of you to offer, but my wife can handle things."

"But she has the kids," I persist. "Besides some of the

123

work might be too heavy for her."

"I appreciate your offer, Jon, but I just don't have any money to pay you with. Maribell will manage."

"I wouldn't expect you to pay me anything. I'd just be doing it to help out—and to help make up for the tractor."

"Forget the tractor. I didn't appreciate what you guys did, but that tractor would've broken down pretty soon without your help. Besides I thought you had a job. What would you do about that?"

"*Had* a job is right. The boss and me didn't see eye to eye on a couple of things."

Dudding smiles. "Got fired, huh? You always were hard to get along with!"

"I guess so. And, letting me work for you would help keep me out of trouble."

"Well, since you put it that way, I guess I could use some help." I walk to the door.

"I'd better let you get your rest. I'll stop by tomorrow and you can tell me what needs to be done."

"Jon," the coach asks, "why are you doing this?"

I flex my muscles. "It's the least I could do. After all, you're responsible for making me the great athlete I am today."

Dudding smiles weakly. "Actually," I add, "I'm finally trying to be the Christian I've claimed to be all along." I wave and duck out into the hall. I look both ways to make sure it's vacant and then I do something I haven't even had the urge to do in a long time—I skip.

* * *

At 7:15 Matt stops by. The Blue Beast already contains the rest of the gang. Matt takes off down the road and I am

124

off for what might be my biggest confrontation of the day.

Chuck is sitting beside Matt giving him directions. We pull into an abandoned lane and come to a clearing by an old barn. Chuck disappears inside the partially collapsed building and emerges triumphantly a few minutes later with a cooler. He sets it down in front of us and opens it. The cooler is packed with ice and malt liquor—the same brand we drank at Indiana Beach.

"For old time's sake," Chuck says. Grinning, he pulls out a can and pops the tab. "Believe me, it wasn't easy getting this stuff." Steve, Denny, and Allen walk over to the cooler and help themselves. Matt and I remain standing where we are.

"Don't be shy," Chuck says. "There's enough to go around."

"No thanks," Matt replies. "We came out here to talk things over—not drink."

Chuck shrugs. "Suit yourselves. That'll just make more for the rest of us."

Chuck finishes his first can, wipes his mouth with his sleeve, pops open another, drops the ring in the can, and makes a toast to friendship. Steve and Denny throw their heads back and swallow long and lustily. Allen takes a sip and sets his beer aside on a tree stump.

The gang begins to reminisce. "We've pulled some good stuff in our time," Steve says. "Remember in study hall how we'd all drop our pencils at the same time. Drove ol' Miss Hanson crazy."

"Yeah," Denny adds, addressing Steve, "and remember when you rolled a metal wastepaper basket down the fire escape during assembly? You got in trouble for that didn't you, Jon?" he asks, turning to me.

Chuck, Steve, and Denny finish their second can and

125

move onto their third. "I tell you," Chuck begins, "women can sure mess up a good thing. I mean, what could be better than our gang? Then look what one woman does to us. Why should we let females ruin everything? Girls may come and girls may go, but we're gonna last forever."

The alcohol is making Chuck talkative. "Good old booze," he says, gazing at his third can. "It'll sure solve a lotta problems for ya. As far as I'm concerned, you can scrap all the schools, churches, and headshrinkers. Just pass around the brew and everything'll be okay. We coulda took care of things in Vietnam once-and-fer-all with a couple million kegs of booze. If we coulda got those little yellow gooks drunk, we woulda taken over the country. Then we coulda sent 'em all to reservations —just like we did with the Injuns." He laughs.

"Yes sir," Matt says, "that's the good old American way." Chuck is not too drunk to catch the sarcasm in Matt's voice. The same alcohol that has made him congenial now causes him to turn surly.

He stumbles toward Matt. "Damn right it is," he says menacingly, poking a finger in Matt's chest. "It sure beats sitting with your hands under your butt and lettin' them commie heathen take over the world." Chuck is in no condition to be reasoned with. Matt doesn't reply, but Chuck isn't ready to let the matter rest.

"I figured you guys would wake up once you grew up and learned how the world really is. But I guess it's once-a-sissy-always-a-sissy." Chuck staggers back to get a view of the whole group. He turns to me, shaking his head to clear his thoughts.

"And you, Jon, you're the biggest sissy of 'em all. If somebody had taken Donna away from me, there woulda been hell to pay. I just can't figure out what kind of man wouldn't lift a finger to keep the prettiest girl in Spireville. But, of course, maybe you're not a man."

"Maybe I just didn't think she was worth fighting about," I reply as calmly as I can.

This remarks draws Steve into the fray. He reels forward. "Whaddya mean not worth fighting about? Are you saying my Donna isn't worth fighting for?"

"It's got nothing to do with Donna. I just don't think any girl is worth fighting over. Besides, fighting doesn't solve anything." Ignoring my last remark, Steve draws closer.

"We're not talking about any girl, we're talking about my Donna who just happens to be the best-lookin' girl in the whole world. I demand an apology."

"Steve, you don't know what you're talking about," I reply. "What you need is to sober up."

"Oh, first Donna's no good and now I'm a drunk," Steve bellows. "Just for that I demand two apologies." He stands swaying in front of me. "Are you gonna 'pologize by yourself or do I have to take 'em out of your hide?"

"Okay, I was wrong. You don't need to sober up. You need to grow up."

Smack! Steve's fist lands beneath my left eye. I lunge at Steve, knocking him to the ground and sending his can of booze flying. We lock arms and roll around clumsily in the dirt.

Oooph! Steve's knee catches me in the stomach. Angrily, I free my right hand and draw it back quickly to strike.

A pair of arms pin me from behind. I struggle for a few seconds—then relax, letting my anger subside. Matt releases his hold on me and helps me to my feet. Chuck grins as he pulls Steve up off the ground.

* * *

Driving home, after the others have been dropped off, Matt rubs salt in my wounds. "Well, Jon," he says, "you sure set a great example tonight for the peaceful resolution of conflict."

"Thanks," I mutter, holding a cold, unopened beer can to my puffy eye. "With you around, who needs a conscience?"

CHAPTER 11

R-r-r-ring, r-r-r-ring.

"Fire!" the chief yells. "Everybody to the trucks." I jump out of bed and into my pants, boots, overcoat, and hat. I grab my monogrammed ax and slide down the pole.

Thud. I wake up in my room on the floor beside my bed.

R-r-r-ring, r-r-r-ring.

"Somebody get that phone!" I yell. No response. The rest of my family must be outside or gone.

R-r-r-ring, r-r-r-ring. I pull on a pair of jeans and head for the phone.

"Hello."

"Hello, is this Jon?"

"No, it's fireman Fred."

"What?"

"Never mind. Yes, it's Jon."

"This is Donna; remember me?"

"Uh, yeah. Hello, Donna."

"I was afraid you hadn't gotten back yet. When did you get home?"

"We got back last night."

"How was your family's vacation?"

"Fine."

"What all did you do?"

"We went fishing, boating, swimming—the usual things." Pause.

"Is something wrong?"

"No, why?"

"You're not saying much."

"Sorry, but just a few minutes ago I was chasing fires in my sleep."

"Oh, did I wake you up?"

"Yeah, but that's okay. In fact I'm glad you did."

"Really? Why?"

"I should be getting over to the Dudding place."

"Oh," Donna replies, her voice falling.

"What time is it anyway?"

"Nine-thirty."

"Shouldn't you be out in the cornfields pulling tassels?"

"We finished last week, thank goodness. If I never see another tassel, it'll be too soon." Pause.

"Did you want something?" I ask.

"Well, I was going to ask you to come over this morning. I don't have anything to do today and it's been a long time since we talked. But, I guess if you're working at Dudding's, that takes care of my question."

"Hey! Why don't you go along with me?" I reprimand myself for sounding too eager.

"Wouldn't I just be in the way?"

"No, there's really not much to do over there right now. We'd have plenty of time to talk. But, of course, it's up to you."

"Well . . . okay, it sounds like fun."

"Great! I'll pick you up in half an hour."

"I'll be waiting."

I stop by for Donna and we drive together to Dudding's farm. I'm glad to see her again, but try not to let it show too much.

At the farm, we hook the water tank to Dudding's new tractor and make the rounds to the various pens. With the main task out of the way, we sit back in the shade of an old cherry tree, watching the cattle drink thirstily in the shimmering August heat.

A cow reaches her head through the fence, straining for the long tufts of grass on the other side. Donna laughs at the comical efforts. "Life's funny, isn't it?" she says. "You always want what you don't have."

"What do you mean by that?" My impression of Donna is that she always knows what she wants and usually gets it.

"Well, when we were going together, I was pretty hung up on Steve. I believed you when we talked about what happened on the Fourth of July. But, I guess I was looking for an excuse to break up."

"You're doing wonders for my ego."

"What I'm trying to say is that after we broke up, I began to realize that I liked you more than I thought—and that I wasn't so sure about Steve. I really missed all the great times we had together."

"Why didn't you say something sooner?"

"I guess it's taken me this long to work up courage."

"Courage? Just to call me up and talk?"

". . . And to let Steve down." Her voice wavers. "He can be awfully possessive."

"What have you told Steve?"

"I haven't told him anything yet. In fact, that's partly what I wanted to see you about."

"What do I have to do with it?"

"Well, when you and I broke up we said it was just for a while. If we'd decide to get back together, I could tell Steve that we were going steady again and he'd have to accept that." She glances over at me quickly, then looks down.

I toy with a blade of foxtail grass, trying to sift through a rush of feelings. I would be lying to myself to say I didn't want to get back with Donna. I've never really gotten her out of my mind since we stopped dating. But, much as I want to believe that she wants to get back together, it seems she only wants to use me again. Before, she wanted to attract Steve by making him jealous; now for some reason she wants to use me to get away from him.

Ironically, I find myself wondering how Sharon would handle the situation. She would get right to the heart of the matter, I decide.

"Donna, what's wrong?" I ask.

"What do you mean?"

"Maybe I'm mistaken, but I think I know you well enough to tell when something's bothering you."

"It shows, huh?"

"Does it have anything to do with Steve?"

Donna nods. "He's changed," she begins. "He used to be so much fun to be around. Now he's always drinking and running around, and when he gets drunk he can really be mean." She fights back a sniffle. "He never takes me anywhere on dates. We just park and . . ." Donna crosses her arms tightly in front of her. "Sometimes he really scares me."

Everything is quiet awhile except for the shuffling and bawling of the cattle. "I'm sorry Donna, I really am. I'll help you anyway I can. I'd talk to Steve except he and I aren't on the best of terms."

"I wouldn't ask you to do that, Jon. I got myself into this and I'll have to get myself out of it. I guess what I needed was for you to listen—and understand."

"You could have gotten the same results without suggesting that we go steady again."

"I guess I was afraid that after all this time you wouldn't want to have anything to do with me. Isn't it strange that it's easier to ask someone to date you than to just be your friend?"

I take her hands in mine and examine them. Her palms and wrists are scarred with minute cuts and scratches.

"My poor hands," Donna moans. "They're a mess, aren't they? And all because I didn't take your advice about soaking them in salt water."

"To tell you the truth," I reply, "the salt water doesn't do much good. Your hands still get cut up."

Donna breaks out into her familiar, musical laughter. "I think there's a moral in there somewhere," she says.

"Toot. Toot."

Coach Dudding's pickup coasts to a stop beside us. The coach gets out and hobbles over to us.

"Sitting down on the job, I see," he says, grinning.

"Can't take a chance on getting sunstroke," I reply.

"In that case, I'll join you." Bracing himself with his crutches he eases himself down onto the ground.

With his beans past cultivation, Bob and I have spent a good bit of time under this same cherry tree. Our conversations have covered almost all imaginable topics, but pacifism has been the most frequent subject. Neither of us has changed much from our original viewpoints— but Dudding has come to respect my beliefs and I've been challenged to work through my own convictions more deeply and carefully.

On several occasions, I've invited Bob and his family to come to the Spireville Mennonite Church. His resistance to the idea has started to waver, but he still hurts from the time that they did attend when they first came to Spireville. He claims that although no one actually snubbed them, they felt like outsiders because they weren't of Mennonite background. After several Sundays they quit coming.

We amuse ourselves by identifying shapes in the puffy clouds that drift lazily across the low sky. "Oh, look at that one," Donna says, pointing. "It looks like a bird of some kind."

"You're right," Bob replies squinting. "I'd say its a red-tailed hawk."

"No," I say, watching the cloud slowly alter its form, "I'd say it's a mourning dove."

After a light lunch—which we barely earned—I drop Donna off and head home.

*   *   *

That evening, Matt stops by for me in the Blue Beast. I climb in and we head for town. He drives slowly, an indication that he wants to tell me something.

"It finally happened," he says.

"What did?"

"We got picked up for drinking."

"You were drinking?"

"No, but I was with the rest of the guys. When I agreed to go out, they claimed they just wanted to shoot some pool. But Chuck got hold of some booze and they all got smashed."

"How'd you get picked up?"

"We were playing ditch-em again, and Denny ran a stop sign."

"And the cop saw him?"

"He couldn't help it. Denny sideswiped him."

"Oh, no!"

"He hauled us into jail and called all our parents. The whole thing got pretty messy."

We ride in silence for awhile. "Aren't we picking anybody else up?" I ask.

"No, our folks aren't too crazy about us hanging around together—so we're coming separately and meeting at the tavern."

"That sounds like a great place to meet—right after you get busted for drinking."

"We'll be on the poolroom side."

As we near the edge of town, Matt muses, almost to himself, "Y'know this might be the last time all summer that the whole gang's together."

"Is that so?"

"Yeah, Denny is leaving tomorrow for two weeks to visit some relatives out East and Chuck and Allen will be on vacation by the time he gets back."

We spot Denny's car parked in front of the tavern and pull up alongside it. Although it's illegal for anyone under 21 to be in the tavern, the only pool tables in town are located there in a side room, and, since it's also the only place open after six o'clock at night in Spireville, the law is overlooked.

Denny and Allen have just finished a game of eight ball when we enter. Matt volunteers to take on the winner while we wait for Steve and Chuck. Allen and I buy Cokes and pull up chairs to watch and shoot the breeze. We shout our conversation over the lively sounds of hollering, jukebox music, and clinking bottles coming from the other side of the tavern.

Denny defeats Matt and I've just challenged Denny when Jack Griffin storms in with Chuck and Steve in tow. They hang back while Jack saunters up to our table, one hand concealed behind his back. It's immediately obvious that none of them are sober. I stand, pool cue in hand, waiting for Jack to say something.

"Go ahead and play," he bellows, planting himself firmly against one side of the table. We begin, but the game is a disaster from the start. With his free hand Jack knocks balls in for Denny and blocks mine from the pockets.

"Jack," I say when I can ignore him no longer, "if you want the winner, you can challenge, but please don't touch the balls." Quickly he snatches a ball off the table and shakes it menacingly at me.

"And what're you gonna do about it if I don't?"

"I'm just asking you, Jack," I reply looking at him.

"Nothing is what you're gonna do, right? You're as big a sissy as they say you are." He gestures toward Steve and Chuck. I try to ignore Jack and concentrate on the pool game. I prepare for my next shot, but as I'm about to shoot Jack nudges my cue stick away.

"Look at that sissy," he taunts, aware that a crowd is gathering. "I hit his cue stick and he doesn't do a damn thing about it. Now if it was me, I'd bust a beer bottle over somebody's head." He turns to his audience and their chuckles egg him on. "And," he continues, "if being a sissy isn't bad enough, I hear he's a cheatin' man too."

"What do you mean by that?" I ask, trying to stay calm.

"I mean that I hear you been goin' out with other people's women. Right?"

136

"Sorry to disappoint you, but you're wrong," I retort.

Steve steps forward. "You liar," he says loudly. "I talked to Donna this afternoon and she said she spent the whole morning with you." Jack pushes Steve back.

"I'm going to ask you one more time," he snarls. "Am I right or wrong?"

"I was with Donna, but according to her she's not Steve's girl. Besides, we just talked."

"I'll bet," he snorts. "Preachers' kids always screw around more'n anybody. Stick their noses in the air like goody-goodies, but run around like the worst hell-raisers in town. Right?" Several onlookers laugh and call encouragement. Jack's callous accusation and the crowd's reaction send a chill through me. I feel like I'm on trial.

Jack abruptly changes the subject. "Where's your older brother these days?"

I'm taken off guard. "Luke?" I say.

"How many older brothers do ya got?"

"Luke's in Wichita," I reply.

"And what's he doing there?" Now I can see what he's driving at. Luke has finished college and is serving two years in Voluntary Service as a social worker in a poor, black section of Wichita, Kansas.

"He's working," I say, stalling.

"What kind of work?" Jack presses.

"Social work."

"Social work, my hind end!" Jack's face darkens. "He's dodging the draft, that's what he's doing."

"He's not dodging the draft," I reply. "He's doing alternative service with poor people in Wichita."

"Poor people! Niggers is what you mean. Not only is he dodging the draft, but he's stirrin' up niggers and incitin' 'em to riot. It does us a hell of a lot of good to fight

137

commies over in Vietnam and then let 'em run free in this country. No wonder everything's goin' to the dogs."

I breathe a silent, almost unconscious prayer for strength and begin to speak. "If this country goes to the dogs," I say, "it won't be because of people like my brother who are willing to help those in need. It'll be because of people like you who are against everything and everybody who doesn't eat, drink, live, and think the same way you do.

"Now wait a minute," Jack cuts in.

"*You* wait a minute," I reply loudly. "You say you believe in this country, but you're not even for the basic things it stands for. You say you're for freedom, but you hate Luke for using his. You say you're for equality but you hate my brother for helping other people try to get theirs. I don't claim to know much about Vietnam, but a lot of people, including Senators and Congressmen who understand more about the situation than either of us, say it's the worst mistake this country ever made." I pause for a moment. The tavern has fallen deathly quiet.

"But," I continue, "mistake or not, my brother wouldn't fight in the war and neither will I. I believe in Jesus Christ and am trying to love all mankind the way he did, not just the ones I happen to take a fancy to. And I've never seen a definition of *love* that includes dropping napalm on people, massacring entire villages, or blowing children's feet off with land mines."

I stop. Jack Griffin looks surprised at my outburst. He glances around the room, then pulls his arm from behind his back. The object he has been hiding turns out to be a rusty pair of scissors. "Maybe what you need is a haircut," he sneers, hesitating. He glances around again. A few people drift away. "That's what they did to Sampson in the

138

Bible when he got too big for his britches. They cut off his hair and put him in his place."

Jack circles me toying with strands of my hair. "I'd be doing you a favor," he says. "Can't tell the girls from the boys these days with their sissy hairstyles." I stand my ground letting Jack do as he pleases.

I hear the scissors snip above my head. Jack steps back triumphantly, holding up a small lock of hair for the crowd's approval. He doesn't get much. People begin to filter back to their tables. Jack makes another try for the spotlight.

"I'm warning you," he bellows so all can hear. "You try coming in here again and we'll throw you out on your heels. Right, men?" No one speaks. Jack struggles to salvage his pride.

"And you stay out of town, too. You keep hangin' around town and . . . and the same thing will happen to you that happened to Denny."

"What happened to Denny?" I ask.

Confidence surges back into Jack's voice. He swells up. "The other night I took the distributor cap from Denny's car and wouldn't give it back until he promised not to be no sissy-tailed CO. And you promised, right, Denny?"

I look over at Denny. He barely nods, eyes glued to the floor.

"Damn right, you promised," Jack speaks for him. Jack glares at me, his face twisted with hate. "You're just lucky we're not out on some dark country road. I'd teach you a lesson you'd never forget—that is if you'd live to remember it." With a last contemptuous look, Jack stalks out of the tavern with Chuck and Steve at his heels.

Quickly the tavern fills with music and laughter as if nothing has happened. A few moments later Denny excuses himself, sprints out of the doorway, gets in his car, and drives away. The rest of us have lost our interest in pool and decide to leave too. Allen asks for a ride home.

After dropping him off, Matt turns the Blue Beast homeward. He pulls into the driveway and stops. We sit silently, both deep in thought. The intensity of the evening's encounter and the heavy loss I feel for Denny well up inside me. Before I know it I am crying.

"Maybe Jack was right about one thing," I say. "I must not be much of a man or I wouldn't cry like this."

"If Jack is the model for being a man," Matt says, "God help us all."

"Well, whatever it means to be a man, I think I've learned something about being a peacemaker."

"What's that?"

"I've learned that to really be a peacemaker you first have to be a follower of Christ. If you make your decisions the way you believe Christ would have, then you'll be ready to face the consequences. I could never have faced Jack alone."

"I know what you mean," Matt replies. "When you try to make decisions on your own, you end up just putting them off. Then, all of a sudden, you realize that each time you thought you were avoiding a decision, you were actually making one—usually the wrong one."

"Yeah, and the thing about wrong decisions is they keep building up until. . . ."

"Ka-plow-ee!" Matt adds with a short laugh. We sit for a moment listening to the distant sounds of the night.

"For some reason," I say, "I feel like I did on graduation night—like part of my life has ended and I'm making a new start. Maybe it's just remembering all we've been through together and realizing things will never be the same again."

"At least we have the option of starting over," Matt says, patting the dashboard of the Blue Beast. "For this contraption it's the end of the line."

"You decided not to take it to college?"

"It's a wonder it lasted this long. With a little luck it'll keep running until we leave for Creston—then it's headed for the junkyard." We talk over school plans until it's time to part.

Avoiding the jagged, protruding springs one last time, I get out and Matt drives away. I stand and watch as the taillights of the Blue Beast grow faint and disappear into the darkness.

CHAPTER 12

Inside the house I find everyone has gone to bed except Dad who is sitting in his favorite chair reading a magazine. He glances up at me as I enter the living room.

"Didn't expect you home this early."

"I didn't expect to *be* home this early."

"Did something happen?"

My first impulse to say no is overridden by a strong urge to level with Dad. "A lot has happened," I say. Dad lays his magazine down.

"Want to tell me about it?"

"I'd like to . . . but I'm not sure I understand it all myself."

"Why don't you give it a try?"

"Okay. . . ." I glance hesitantly down the hall toward the open bedroom doors.

"Why don't we go into the study," Dad suggests. He follows me into the small, book-lined room and closes the door. Dad eases into his cushioned chair and I take one of the hard seats across the desk from him. He leans back, swiveling slightly from side to side, waiting for me to speak. I squirm uncomfortably, trying to sort out my thoughts and feelings.

"So much has happened I don't know where to begin," I say.

"Where would you like to begin?"

"Well, I suppose the trip to Indiana Beach is as good a place as any." While Dad listens, I fill him in on my activities of the summer—the escapades at Indiana Beach, the tricks on Dudding, the drinking, my relationship with Donna, and the problems in the gang. Finally I bring him up to date with the confrontation in the tavern.

When I finish I feel a great sense of release—like a heavy burden that I've carried a long time has been lightened. I pause a moment to catch my breath.

"A lot of this probably comes as quite a shock to you," I add.

"No, not really," Dad says calmly.

"You mean you've known all along?"

"Let's say I had a pretty good idea about most of it."

"How'd you find out?"

"Small towns don't keep many secrets. And, to be honest, I was eighteen once myself."

"If you knew, why didn't you say something before?"

"Would you have been ready to talk before?" We sit a few moments in silence.

"You seem to have given some thought to the things you did that were wrong," Dad continues. "Have you given any thought to what you're going to do about it?"

"Some. I know that I want Christ in my life no matter what. Things get too tangled up otherwise. Maybe that means I should be baptized. . . ."

"But you've been baptized."

"When I was 12 and too young to know what I was doing."

"I remember a determined 12-year-old boy who claimed he knew exactly what he was doing."

"All that's happened since seems to prove that I didn't."

"The way I see it, you've compromised your faith—giving in to group pressure and following your own self-centered desires. But your faith in Christ eventually won out."

"Well, isn't that a reason for baptism—to show that I've changed and am now ready to follow Christ?"

"You were baptized when you expressed a desire to begin your Christian pilgrimage. It wasn't a guarantee then, and it wouldn't be now. You'll face a whole new set of experiences before you're 25. And, being human, you'll likely make some more wrong decisions. Will you want to get baptized again then?

"I'm not saying for certain you shouldn't be rebaptized," Dad continues. "If you really believe your first baptism was insincere, our church would probably agree to baptize you again. But whether or not you are rebaptized is the easiest part of this matter."

"What do you mean?"

"Well, let me use your process of registering for the draft as an example. Deciding to ask for 1-0 status was a big step in that it signified your desire to become a peacemaker. But you didn't really become a peacemaker until you could put your beliefs into action—the way you did by helping Bob Dudding. The same principles apply here. Baptism is important for signifying commitment to Christ, but it's how you live out that commitment that counts. Do you understand what I'm saying?"

"I understand what you're saying, but I'm not sure what it all means."

"First you need to understand that your sin was not so

144

much what you did, but what you didn't do as part of the church. The community of believers is Christ's presence on earth. Each member of this body must function in harmonious relationship with the other members. At age 12 you chose to identify with the body of Christ—but failed to maintain the necessary relationships. If you now wish to function as part of the community of faith, I believe you'll need to ask forgiveness and begin reestablishing the proper relationships. How you do this will be up to you. I'd suggest giving the matter a lot of prayer."

I study the wood grain on the side of the desk for a minute or two, then look up. "Could I say something to the congregation on Sunday morning—about what I've done and what I believe now?"

"That might be a good start. It would let the other members know how your feel. If you're to follow Christ faithfully, you'll need their support. . . ." Dad is unable to suppress a yawn.

"I may have been eighteen once," he says, "but I'm not anymore. It's past my bedtime. Why don't we talk more tomorrow?" We stand to leave.

"Thanks for taking the time to talk," I say.

"I was glad to do it," Dad replies, "as your father, *and* as a brother in the church." Dad begins to pat me on the shoulder, changes his mind, and shakes my hand firmly instead.

"Just out of curiosity," Dad says as we turn down the hall, "how are you coming on your conscientious objector form? If you're stuck on any of the questions, I'll be glad to help."

"You already have," I reply.

In my room I clear a place on my desk and open the

long-neglected form to Question 4. I read it over once more: "Have you ever given expression, publicly or privately, written or oral, to the views herein expressed as the basis for your claim?"

I reflect for a minute on what Dad said—that your beliefs are expressed more by your actions than your words. I think about my own actions—my reconciliation with Coach Dudding and my confrontation with Jack in the tavern. In both instances I tried to act as I believe Christ would have—as a peacemaker.

I spread the form out on the desk, take a pen, and begin to write.

AUTHOR'S POSTSCRIPT

Once a manuscript is finished, the hardest decision an author yet faces is to whom to dedicate the book. I have decided not to dedicate this book to any one person since I would have to choose between my wife, Nancy, for typing the manuscript and putting up with my frequent absences, my grandparents for letting me hole up in their basement for a week while I labored through a second draft, Dan Shenk for his extensive and energetic editing, or Paul M. Schrock, book editor for Herald Press, who always answered my garbled, scribbled letters with neat, organized ones.

Instead I would like to dedicate this book to all members of the Historic Peace Churches in general, and the Mennonite Church in particular, whose convictions were severely tested by the draft and the Vietnam War. Those of us who turned 18 during that eight-year span were affected by a turbulent era that we will think and talk about for the rest of our lives.

I would also like to dedicate this book to those who come after us and are doomed to be bored to tears by our stories and recollections of this era for most of the rest of their lives. They are doomed not only to hear our stories but to have their "ignorance and apathy" of peacemaking constantly compared to my generation's "deep insights and involvement" with the issue.

I wrote this book because I firmly believe that we as Christian believers *do* need to keep talking about peace and our experiences as peacemakers. Otherwise we face the danger of being lulled to sleep with the notion that peacemaking is inherent in our nature. A simple history lesson of Mennonite participation in the Civil War will dispel that notion.

But, while there is danger in not reflecting on our experiences as peacemakers, there can also be danger in *how* we do that reflection. The temptation is to recount selectively tales of conscientious objectors courageously confronting the establishment. This approach alone, in my opinion, is not only less than helpful to modern-day pacifists, it is less than truthful.

Although the response by pacifists to the draft and war was at times courageous, it was just as often confused, comatose, or even cowardly. While some persons did go to jail, to Canada, or into Voluntary (alternate) Service, many simply went to college—and stayed there. We did join a notable parade of Anabaptist ancestry in protesting war, but we were the first to do so in an era when such protest was not only acceptable, but prestigious. And, ironically, while the struggle of our Anabaptist forebearers placed them in physical peril, our stance as conscientious objectors kept us safe from such peril.

While we faced few persecutions, we did face some hard choices. We had to make the choice between conscientious objector or soldier. We had to choose to accept or reject our long—if spotted—heritage of peacemaking. And, ultimately,

Sisters and Brothers
by Joel Kauffmann

we had to make a choice about what it means to follow Christ.

Choosing whether or not to follow Christ was the central element of peacemaking that we of my generation shared with those who came before us, and share with those who come after us. It seemed to me like the one thing most worth writing about.

I picked the title *The Weight* because I believe it best expresses both the heaviness and importance of these decisions for a person 18 years of age. Weight also suggests the need for having a firm foundation when making such decisions. It should be noted that the vast majority of persons in our society whose convictions were not founded in Christ lost interest in peacemaking when the draft no longer threatened their own well-being.

I hope that after reading this book you have a greater appreciation for the peacemaking response of my generation to the world that we experienced. My greater hope is that you have gained understanding into what your peacemaking response should be to the world in which you are now living.

Joel Kauffmann
Elkhart, Indiana

Photo by Howard Zehr, Jr.

Joel Kauffmann grew up two miles outside Hopedale, Illinois. He recalls that the town belonged to the Protestants and Catholics and the Mennonites owned the land around it.

After high school, he went to Hesston College, Hesston, Kansas, where he spent two years maintaining a B average and watching the Vietnam protest movement crest. Disillusioned with church, school, and society, he found a job as a farmhand in the desolate stretches of western Kansas. After several months, his boss became disillusioned with him and kindly suggested that he try something else.

In 1972, after stints as a gas station attendant and

meat-packer, Joel began working in the communication department of Mennonite Board of Missions, Elkhart, Indiana. Since then he has finished college (Goshen), married, become the father of two children, started the cartoon strip, "Sisters and Brothers," and grown a beard. Joel and his wife, Nancy, are involved in the Prairie Street Mennonite Church and served as youth sponsors there for four years.

Joel's own experience with the draft was turbulent. He was denied 1-0 status by the local draft board and the state board of appeals. He was granted 1-0 status by the presidential board of appeals only after the Supreme Court ruled in the Cassius Clay case that certain criteria, such as sincerity, could not be used to deny persons 1-0 status. Lack of sincerity, it seems, was a popular excuse used by Illinois draft boards.

Joel suggests that persons interested in studying a current Mennonite Church statement on "Militarism and Conscription" request a copy of that document from Mennonite Board of Congregational Ministries, Box 1245, Elkhart, IN 46515.